May. 2013

THE SMURFLINGS

Peyo

WITHDRAWN

THE
SMURFLINGS

A **SMURFS** GRAPHIC NOVEL BY *Peyo*

PAPERCUTZ™
NEW YORK

SMURFS GRAPHIC NOVELS AVAILABLE FROM PAPERCUTZ™

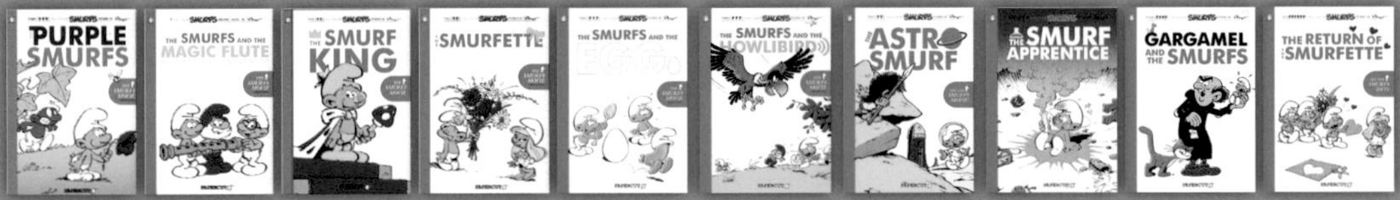
PURPLE SMURFS
THE SMURFS AND THE MAGIC FLUTE
THE SMURF KING
SMURFETTE
THE SMURFS AND THE
THE SMURFS AND THE HOWLIBIRD
ASTRO SMURF
THE SMURF APPRENTICE
GARGAMEL AND THE SMURFS
THE RETURN OF THE SMURFETTE

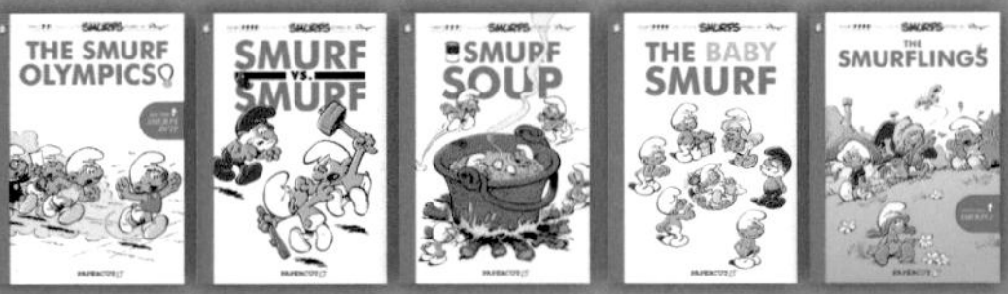
THE SMURF OLYMPICS
SMURF VS. SMURF
SMURF SOUP
THE BABY SMURF
THE SMURFLINGS

1. THE PURPLE SMURFS
2. THE SMURFS AND THE MAGIC FLUTE
3. THE SMURF KING
4. THE SMURFETTE
5. THE SMURFS AND THE EGG
6. THE SMURFS AND THE HOWLIBIRD
7. THE ASTROSMURF
8. THE SMURF APPRENTICE
9. GARGAMEL AND THE SMURFS
10. THE RETURN OF THE SMURFETTE
11. THE SMURF OLYMPICS
12. SMURF VS. SMURF
13. SMURF SOUP
14. THE BABY SMURF
15. THE SMURFLINGS

COMING SOON:

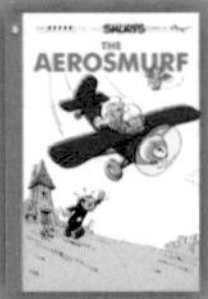
THE AEROSMURF

16. **THE AEROSMURF**

THE SMURFS graphic novels are available in paperback for $5.99 each and in hardcover for $10.99 each at booksellers everywhere. You can also order online at www.papercutz.com. Or call 1-800-886-1223, Monday through Fridays, 9 – 5 EST. MC, Visa, and AmEx accepted. To order by mail, please add $4.00 for postage and handling for first book ordered, $1.00 for each additional book and make check payable to NBM Publishing. Send to: Papercutz, 160 Broadway, Suite 700, East Wing, New York, NY 10038.

THE SMURFS graphic novels are also available digitally wherever e-books are sold.

WWW.PAPERCUTZ.COM

THE SMURFLINGS

"The Smurflings"
BY PEYO

"Puppy and the Smurfs"
BY PEYO

"The Smurfs and the Little Ghosts"
BY PEYO

"The Smurfs and the Booglooboo"
BY PEYO

Joe Johnson, *SMURFLATIONS*
Adam Grano, *SMURFIC DESIGN*
Janice Chiang, *LETTERING SMURFETTE*
Matt. Murray, *SMURF CONSULTANT*
Beth Scorzato, *SMURF COORDINATOR*
Michael Petranek, *ASSOCIATE SMURF*
Jim Salicrup, *SMURF-IN-CHIEF*

PAPERBACK EDITION ISBN: 978-1-59707-407-0
HARDCOVER EDITION ISBN: 978-1-59707-408-7

PRINTED IN CHINA FEBRUARY 2013 BY WKT CO. LTD.
3/F PHASE I LEADER INDUSTRIAL CENTRE
188 TEXACO ROAD, TSEUN WAN, N.T., HONG KONG

Papercutz books may be purchased for business or promotional use. For information on bulk purchases please contact Macmillan Corporate and Premium Sales Department at (800) 221-7945 x5442.

DISTRIBUTED BY MACMILLAN
FIRST PAPERCUTZ PRINTING

THE SMURFLINGS

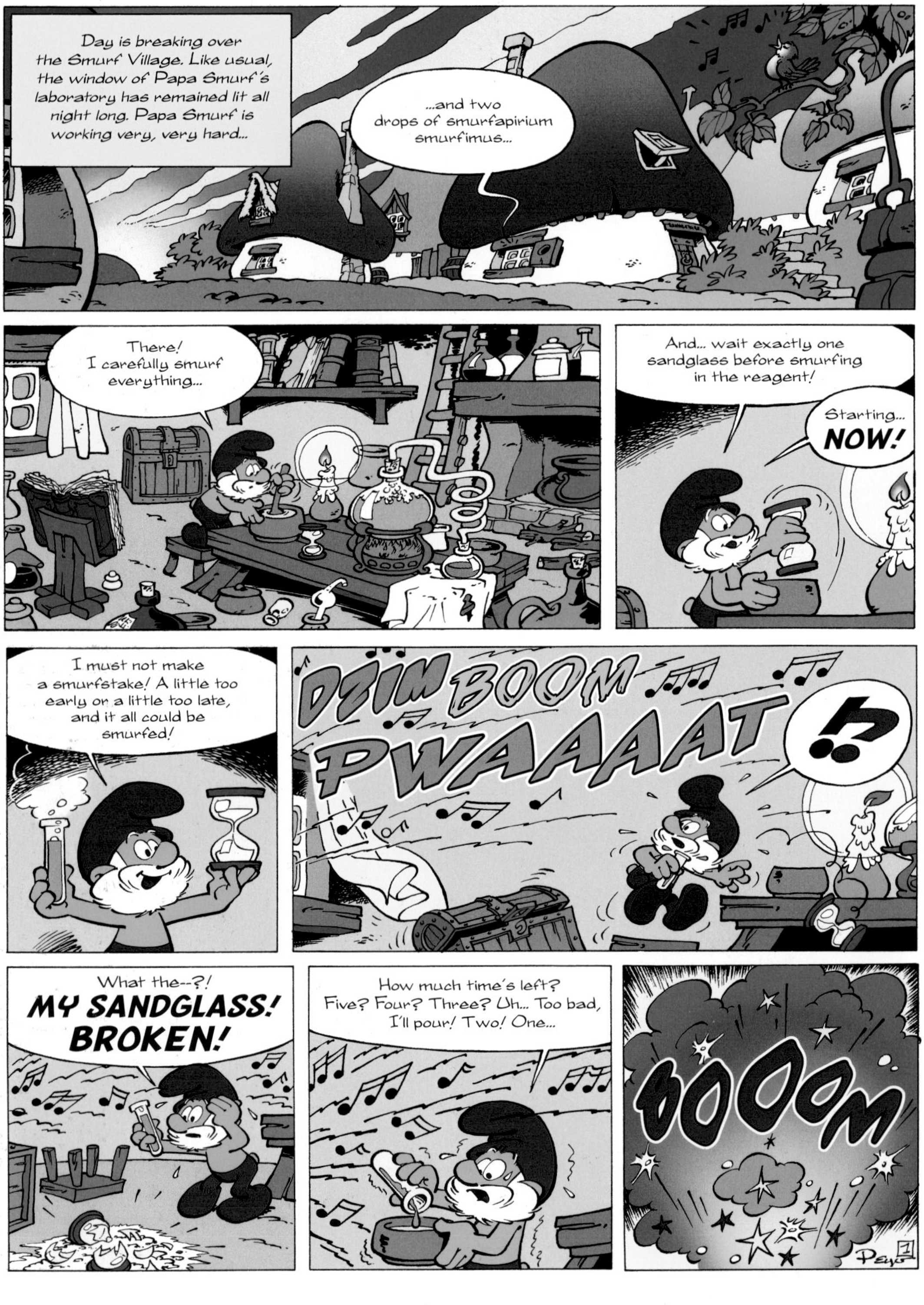

Day is breaking over the Smurf Village. Like usual, the window of Papa Smurf's laboratory has remained lit all night long. Papa Smurf is working very, very hard...
...and two drops of smurfapirium smurfimus...
There! I carefully smurf everything...
And... wait exactly one sandglass before smurfing in the reagent!
Starting... NOW!
I must not make a smurfstake! A little too early or a little too late, and it all could be smurfed!
DZIM BOOM
PWAAAAT
!?
What the--?! MY SANDGLASS! BROKEN!
How much time's left? Five? Four? Three? Uh... Too bad, I'll pour! Two! One...
BOOOM

OOMPAOOMPAOOMPAH...

going on?

...ey've gone completely smurfers!

...AAATEERELE...EETEERELE...

LABORATORY

!

DZIMBOOM TIROOM POO

Ah! It's you, Papa Smurf!

What's all this ruck... Are yo... crazy?

LILA PWAAATPWEEE DINGELINGELLONG

...because ...d sm...f! ...aha... Wha... ...can't gotten into you-- understand making all you! this racket?

♪ ENOUGH!

WEOOEE... ♪

What the smurf's got you smurfing music at this hour?

But, Papa Smurf, we're rehearsing! We're smurfing a big concert tonight! Remember?

Ah! Hmm! That's right! Uh, okay, continue!

Good! Let's take it from the top... Smurf, two, three...

Meanwhile, my experiment is ruined! And... I don't even have a sandglass left!

Hey! Snappy Smurf, Natural Smurf, and Slouchy Smurf! That gives me an idea!

Your @$&# butterfly's making me mad!

But Butterfly's nice!

Yep!

Peyo

2

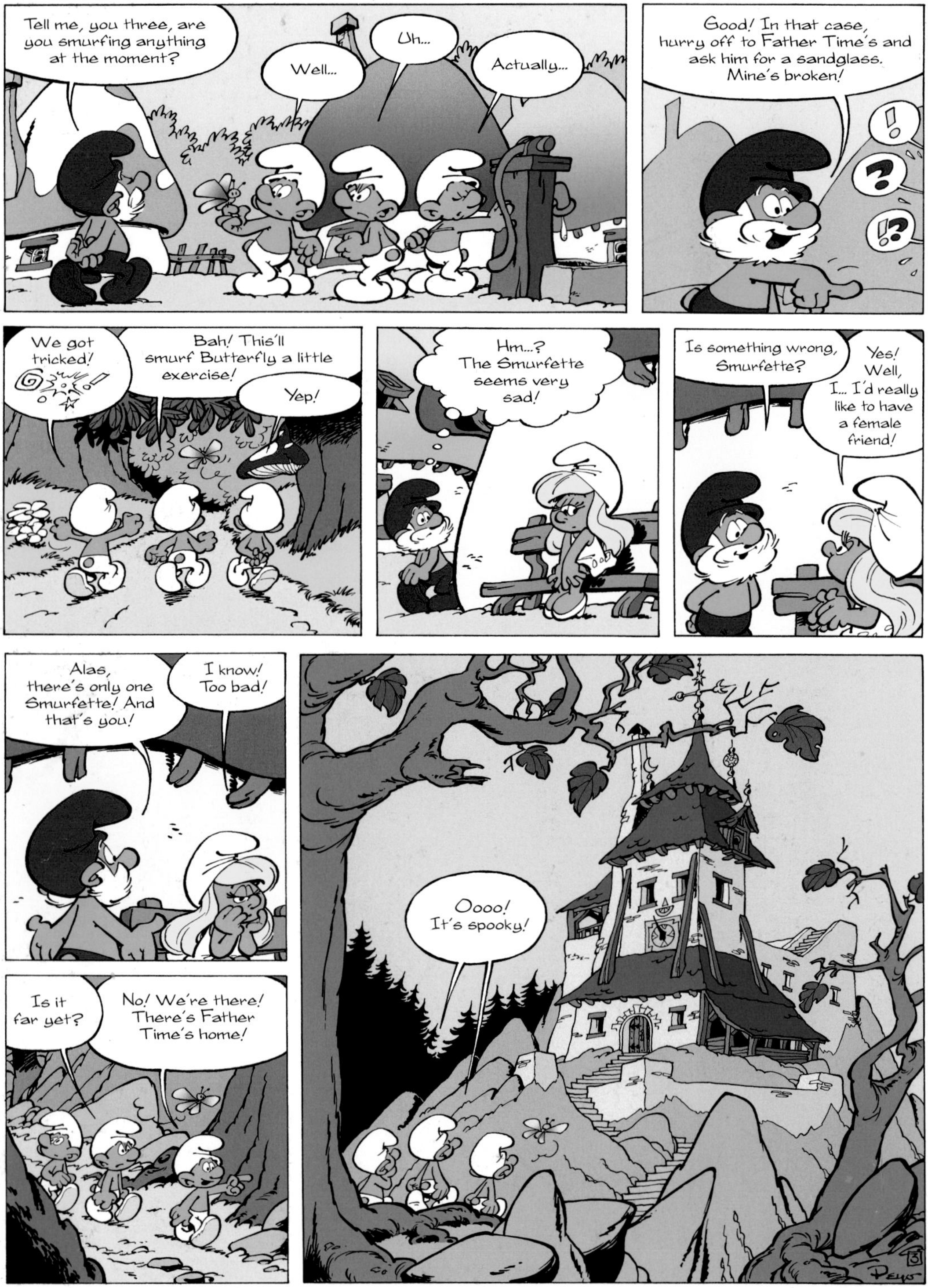

Tell me, you three, are you smurfing anything at the moment?
Well...
Uh...
Actually...
Good! In that case, hurry off to Father Time's and ask him for a sandglass. Mine's broken!
!
?
!?
We got tricked!
Bah! This'll smurf Butterfly a little exercise!
Yep!
Hm...? The Smurfette seems very sad!
Is something wrong, Smurfette?
Yes! Well, I... I'd really like to have a female friend!
Alas, there's only one Smurfette! And that's you!
I know! Too bad!
Is it far yet?
No! We're there! There's Father Time's home!
Oooo! It's spooky!

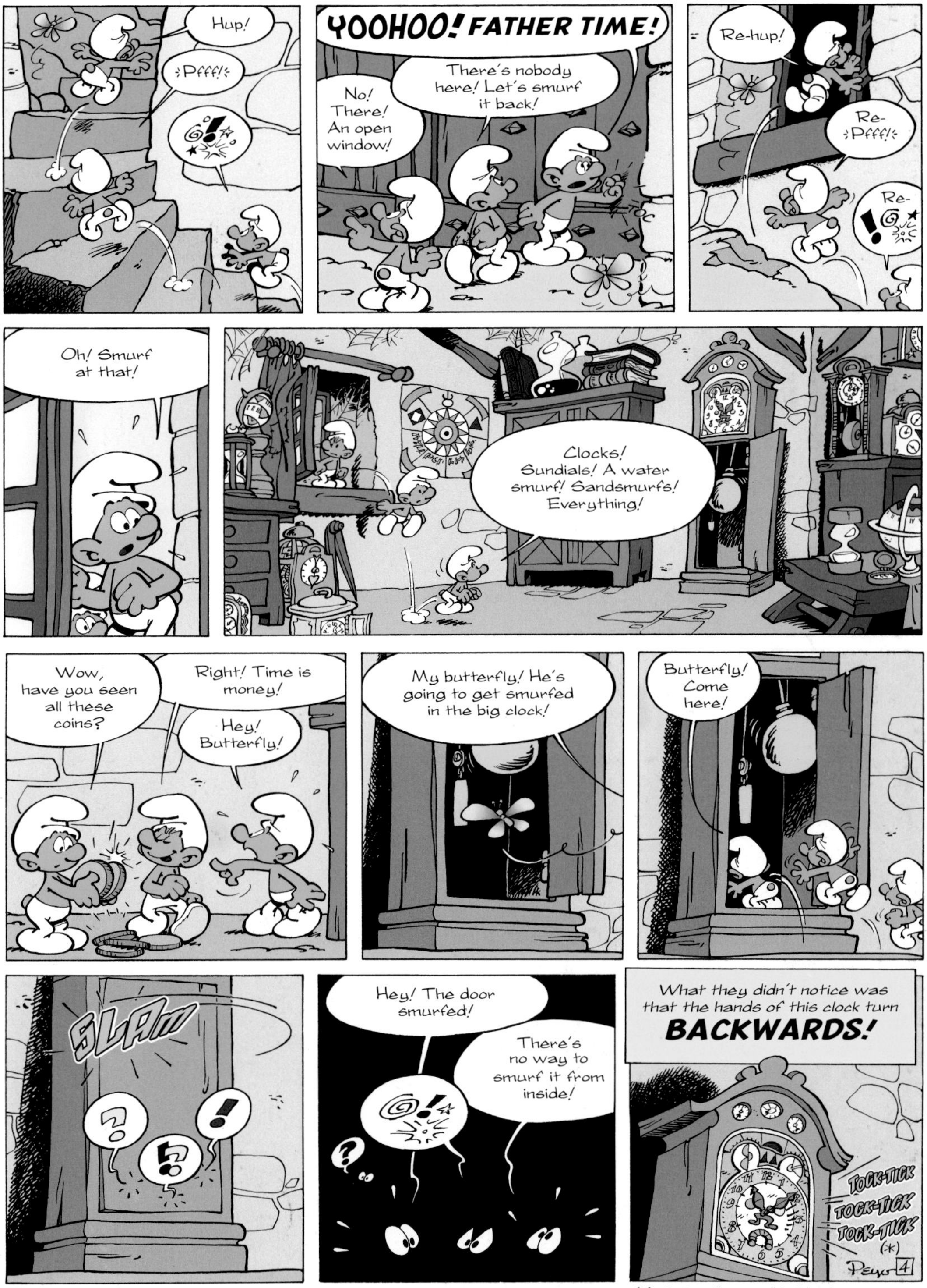
Hup!
Pfff!
YOOHOO! FATHER TIME!
No! There! An open window!
There's nobody here! Let's smurf it back!
Re-hup!
Re-Pfff!
Re-
Oh! Smurf at that!
Clocks! Sundials! A water smurf! Sandsmurfs! Everything!
Wow, have you seen all these coins?
Right! Time is money!
Hey! Butterfly!
My butterfly! He's going to get smurfed in the big clock!
Butterfly! Come here!
SLAM
Hey! The door smurfed!
There's no way to smurf it from inside!
What they didn't notice was that the hands of this clock turn BACKWARDS!
TOCK-TICK
TOCK-TICK
TOCK-TICK
(*)
Peyo 4

(*) And not "tick-tock" (--Editor)

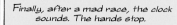

Suddenly, the hands start spinning, turning faster and faster. And always in reverse...

DONG DING
TOCK-TICK
TOCK TICK TOCK
BONG

Finally, after a mad race, the clock sounds. The hands stop.

BONG

The door opens and...

CLIP

What happened?

I don't know!

I feel all strange!

That's funny! Our clothes have gotten too big!

No--I think we've become smaller,

And where's Butterfly?

Hee hee hee! Butterfly! You've gotten younger, too! You've become a caterpillar again!

All right! What do we do? Do we wait for Father Time so he can smurf us back to our normal size?

Why? Does it bother you being Smurflings?

No!

Okay then, let's go back!

Yes, but you're forgetting Papa Smurf's sandglass!

Bah! We'll take one and leave a note!

I'm curious to see the other Smurfs' faces once they smurf us!

Hee hee hee! Me, too!

If they make smurf of us, I'm going to smurf mad!

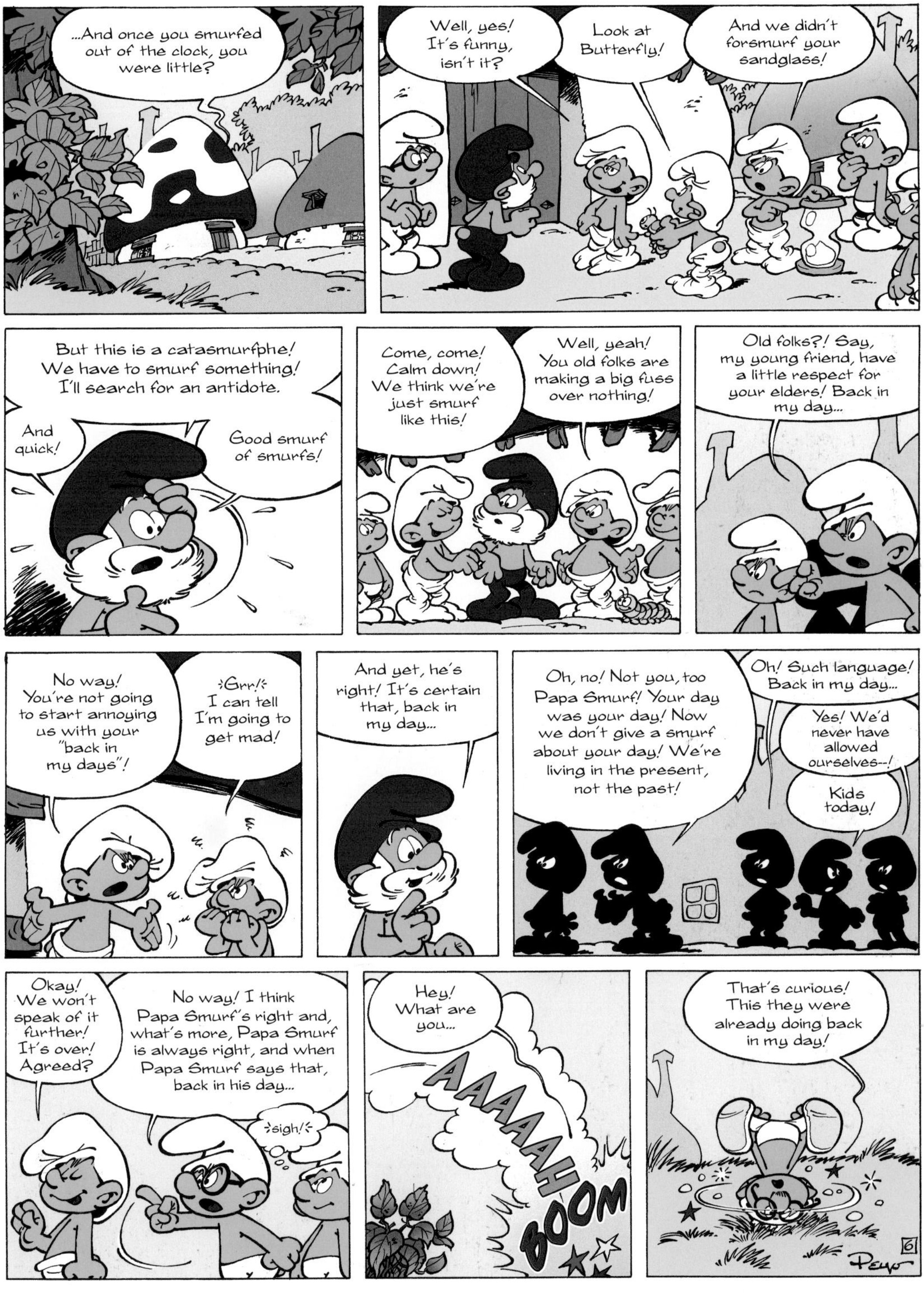
...And once you smurfed out of the clock, you were little?
Well, yes! It's funny, isn't it?
Look at Butterfly!
And we didn't forsmurf your sandglass!
But this is a catasmurfphe! We have to smurf something! I'll search for an antidote.
And quick!
Good smurf of smurfs!
Come, come! Calm down! We think we're just smurf like this!
Well, yeah! You old folks are making a big fuss over nothing!
Old folks?! Say, my young friend, have a little respect for your elders! Back in my day...
No way! You're not going to start annoying us with your "back in my days"!
Grr! I can tell I'm going to get mad!
And yet, he's right! It's certain that, back in my day...
Oh, no! Not you, too Papa Smurf! Your day was your day! Now we don't give a smurf about your day! We're living in the present, not the past!
Oh! Such language! Back in my day...
Yes! We'd never have allowed ourselves--!
Kids today!
Okay! We won't speak of it further! It's over! Agreed?
No way! I think Papa Smurf's right and, what's more, Papa Smurf is always right, and when Papa Smurf says that, back in his day...
sigh!
Hey! What are you...
AAAAAH
BOOM
That's curious! This they were already doing back in my day!
6
Peyo

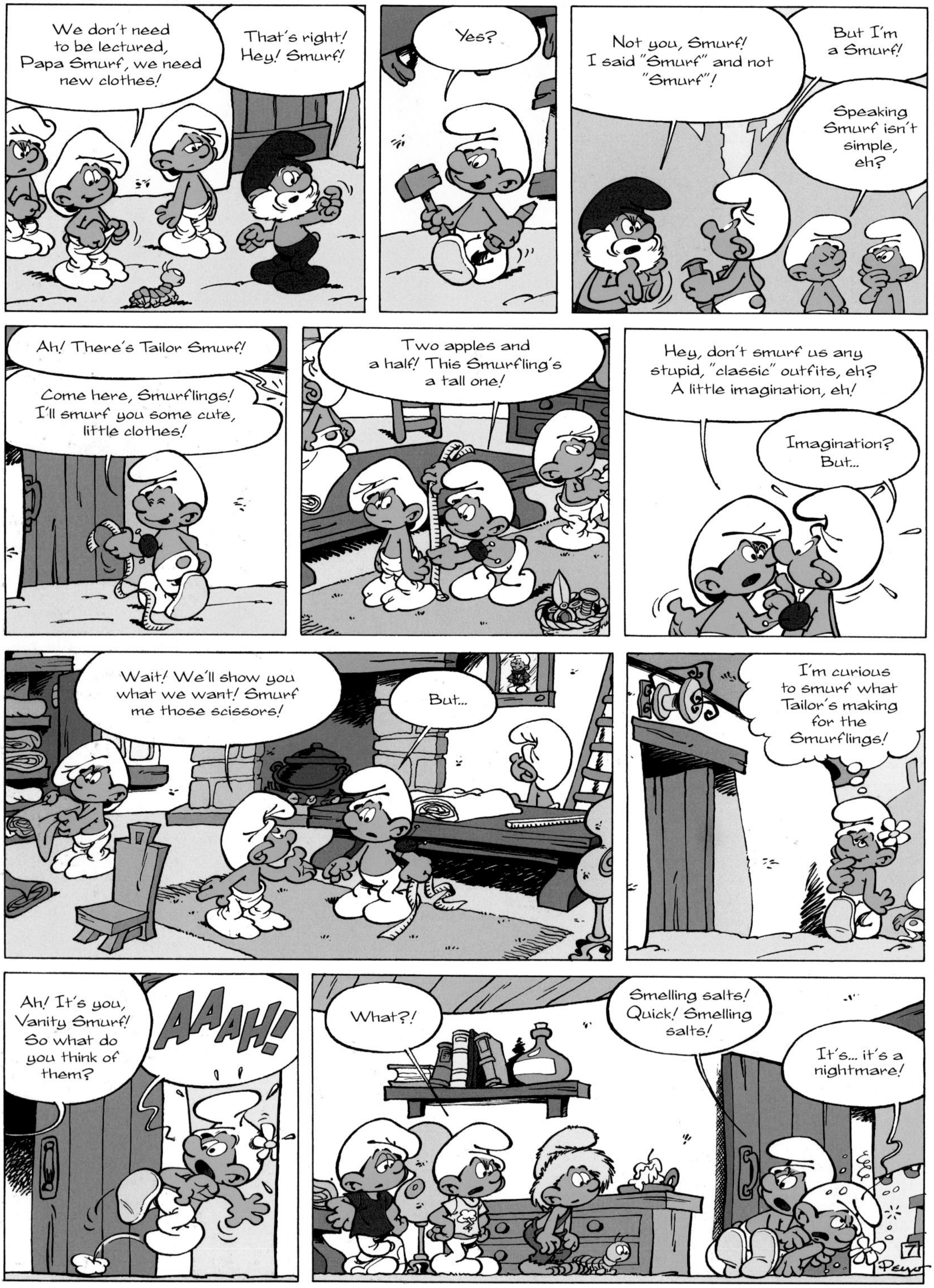
We don't need to be lectured, Papa Smurf, we need new clothes!
That's right! Hey! Smurf!
Yes?
Not you, Smurf! I said "Smurf" and not "Smurf"!
But I'm a Smurf!
Speaking Smurf isn't simple, eh?
Ah! There's Tailor Smurf!
Come here, Smurflings! I'll smurf you some cute, little clothes!
Two apples and a half! This Smurfling's a tall one!
Hey, don't smurf us any stupid, "classic" outfits, eh? A little imagination, eh!
Imagination? But...
Wait! We'll show you what we want! Smurf me those scissors!
But...
I'm curious to smurf what Tailor's making for the Smurflings!
Ah! It's you, Vanity Smurf! So what do you think of them?
AAAH!
What?!
Smelling salts! Quick! Smelling salts!
It's... it's a nightmare!
7
Peyo

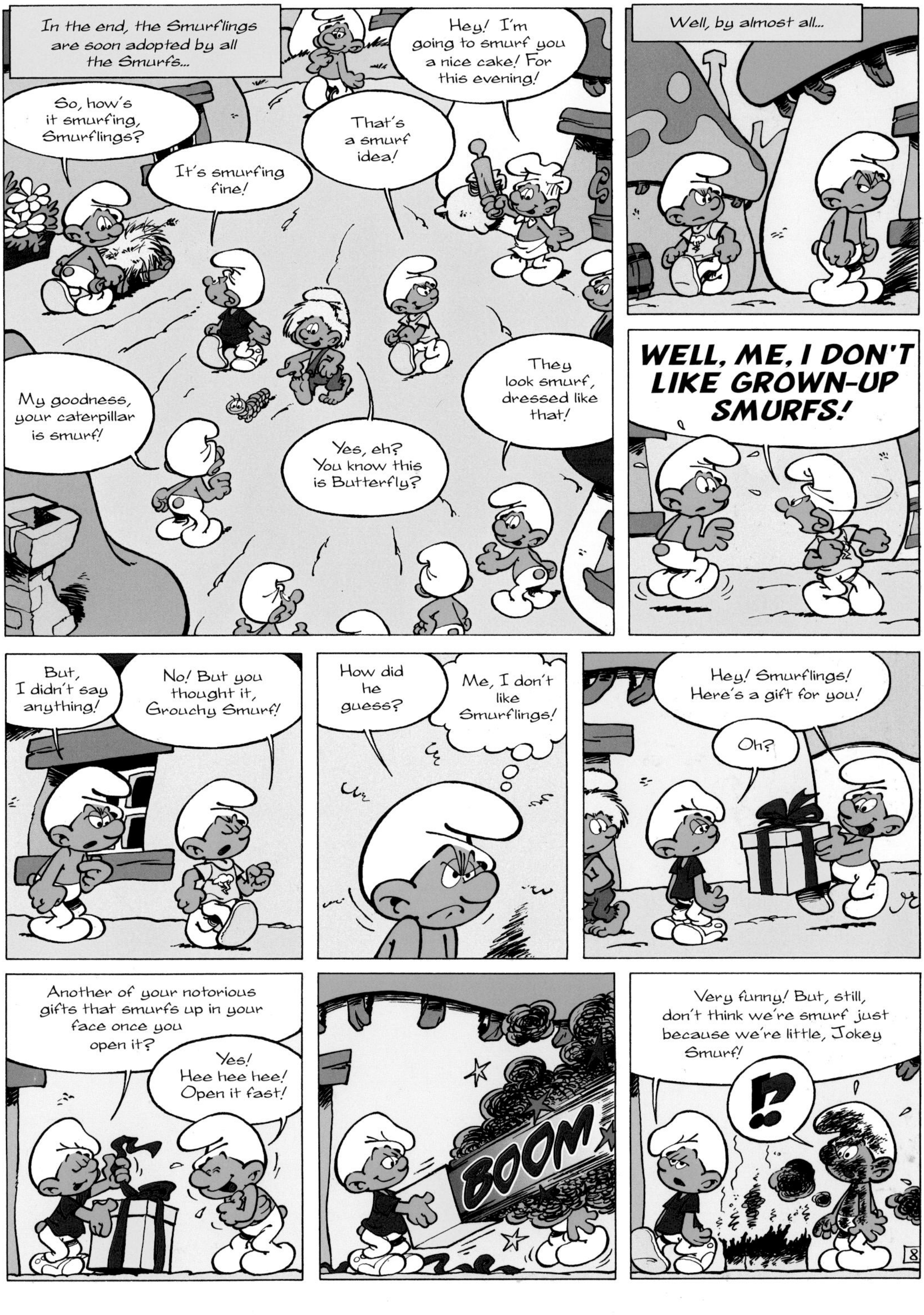
In the end, the Smurflings are soon adopted by all the Smurfs...
So, how's it smurfing, Smurflings?
It's smurfing fine!
That's a smurf idea!
Hey! I'm going to smurf you a nice cake! For this evening!
My goodness, your caterpillar is smurf!
Yes, eh? You know this is Butterfly?
They look smurf, dressed like that!
Well, by almost all...
WELL, ME, I DON'T LIKE GROWN-UP SMURFS!
But, I didn't say anything!
No! But you thought it, Grouchy Smurf!
How did he guess?
Me, I don't like Smurflings!
Hey! Smurflings! Here's a gift for you!
Oh?
Another of your notorious gifts that smurfs up in your face once you open it?
Yes! Hee hee hee! Open it fast!
BOOM
Very funny! But, still, don't think we're smurf just because we're little, Jokey Smurf!
8

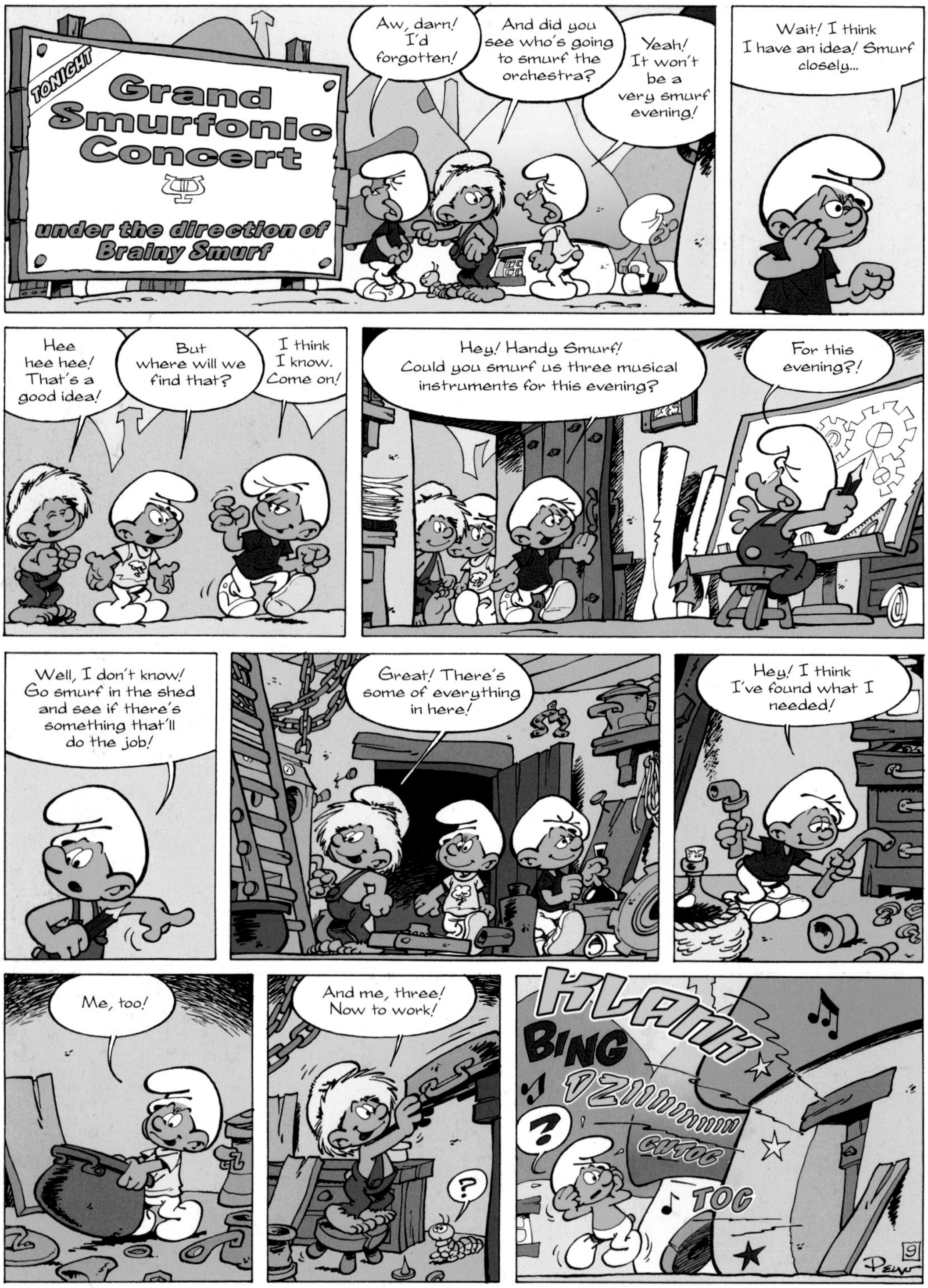
TONIGHT
Grand Smurfonic Concert
under the direction of Brainy Smurf
Aw, darn! I'd forgotten!
And did you see who's going to smurf the orchestra?
Yeah! It won't be a very smurf evening!
Wait! I think I have an idea! Smurf closely...
Hee hee hee! That's a good idea!
But where will we find that?
I think I know. Come on!
Hey! Handy Smurf! Could you smurf us three musical instruments for this evening?
For this evening?!
Well, I don't know! Go smurf in the shed and see if there's something that'll do the job!
Great! There's some of everything in here!
Hey! I think I've found what I needed!
Me, too!
And me, three! Now to work!
?
KLANK
BING
DZIIIIIiiiiiiii
CLITOC
TOC
?
9

Oh, hey! Papa Smurf!

We'd like to play tonight, too! Can we?

Look! We have everything we need!

Say yes!

Well, uh... it's just... Oh! And then, after all, why not?

YIPPEE!

We have just enough time to practice some harmonizing!

I like it when youngsters smurf the initiative!

Start without me! I'm going to drop by Poet Smurf's!

You wouldn't have a little glue?

Well, yes!

TONIGHT Grand Smurfonic Conc... With the group "THE SMURFLINGS" unde... ...ion of B...nny Smurf

Papa Smurf! Papa Smurf! Did you see? The Smurflings want to smurf music, too!

So what? That's their right! In the land of the Smurfs, everyone is free to smurf as he likes!

Fine! Fine! Let them smurf! But we'll see who gets the last smurf!

And that evening...

Mezzo vivace, allegro ma non troppo!

Lazy Smurf! Wake up! You're snoring!

Huh? What?! But I'm not Lazy Smurf!

Oh? Sorry...

Voila! That'll bring the house down with applause!

Hmm... And now for something in a different style: meet **THE SMURFLINGS!**

Why, yes! Go ahead, kids! The tomatoes will soon be smurfing! Hee hee hee!

One... two... one-two-three-four...

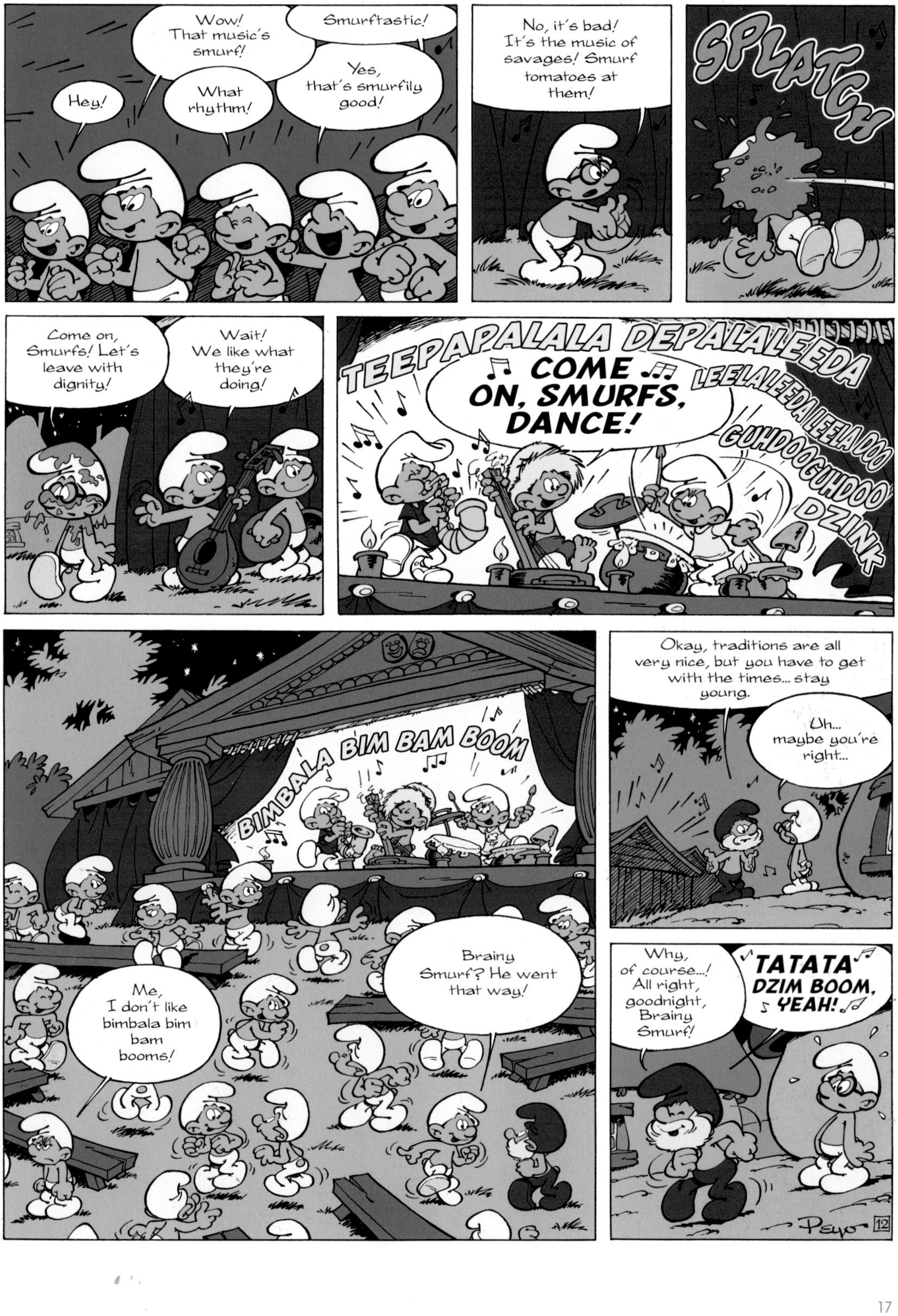
Hey!
Wow! That music's smurf!
What rhythm!
Smurftastic!
Yes, that's smurfily good!
No, it's bad! It's the music of savages! Smurf tomatoes at them!
SPLATCH
Come on, Smurfs! Let's leave with dignity!
Wait! We like what they're doing!
TEEPAPALALA DEPALALEEDA
COME ON, SMURFS, DANCE!
LEELALEEDA LEELA DOO
GUHDOO GUHDOO
DZINK
BIMBALA BIM BAM BOOM
Me, I don't like bimbala bim bam booms!
Brainy Smurf? He went that way!
Okay, traditions are all very nice, but you have to get with the times... stay young.
Uh... maybe you're right...
Why, of course...! All right, goodnight, Brainy Smurf!
TATATA DZIM BOOM, YEAH!
Peyo
12

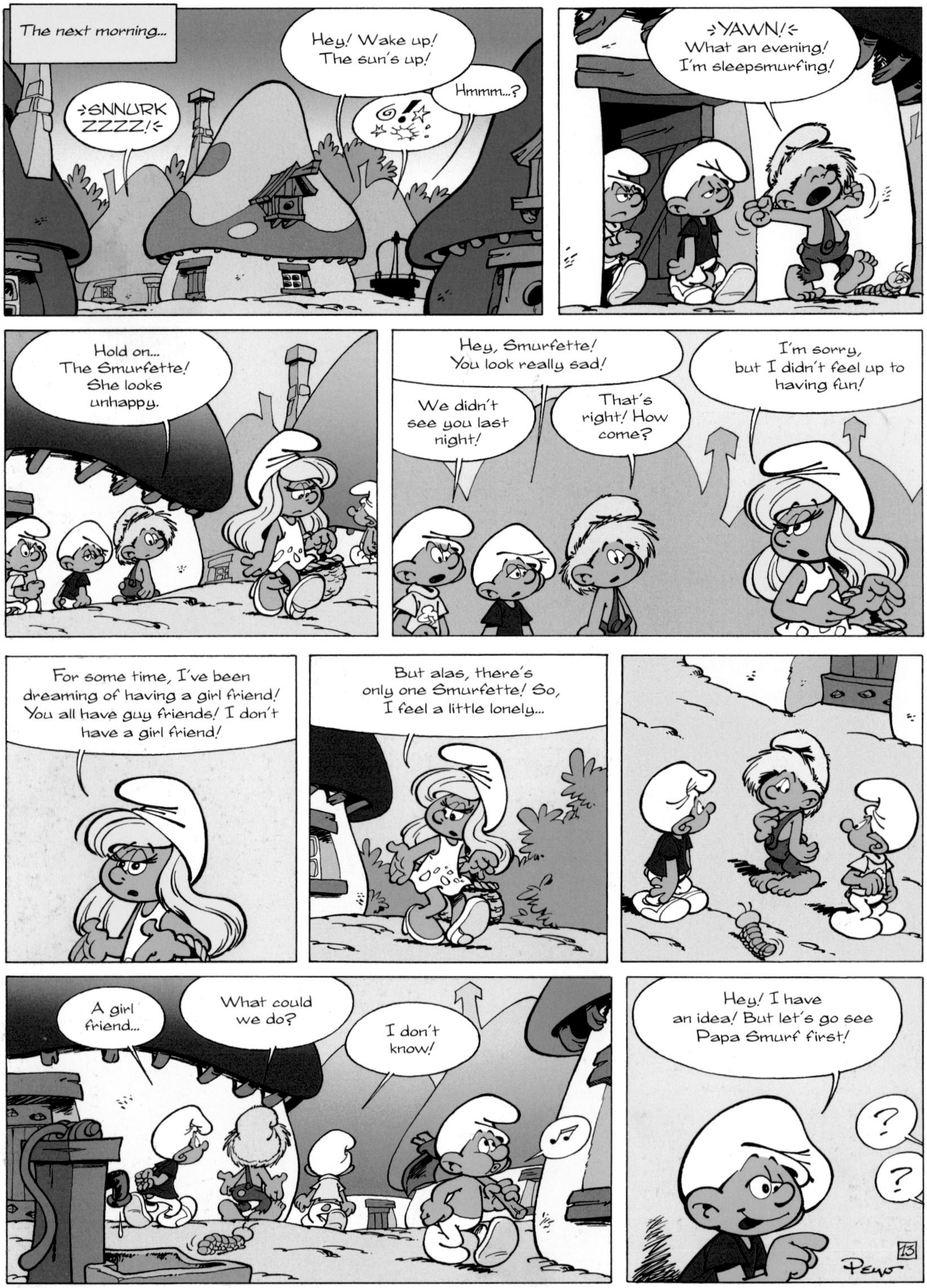

The next morning...
⁘SNNURK ZZZZ!⁘
Hey! Wake up! The sun's up!
Hmmm...?
⁘YAWN!⁘ What an evening! I'm sleepsmurfing!
Hold on... The Smurfette! She looks unhappy.
Hey, Smurfette! You look really sad!
We didn't see you last night!
That's right! How come?
I'm sorry, but I didn't feel up to having fun!
For some time, I've been dreaming of having a girl friend! You all have guy friends! I don't have a girl friend!
But alas, there's only one Smurfette! So, I feel a little lonely...
A girl friend...
What could we do?
I don't know!
Hey! I have an idea! But let's go see Papa Smurf first!
?
?
13
Peyo

(✳) See THE SMURFS #4 "The Smurfette"

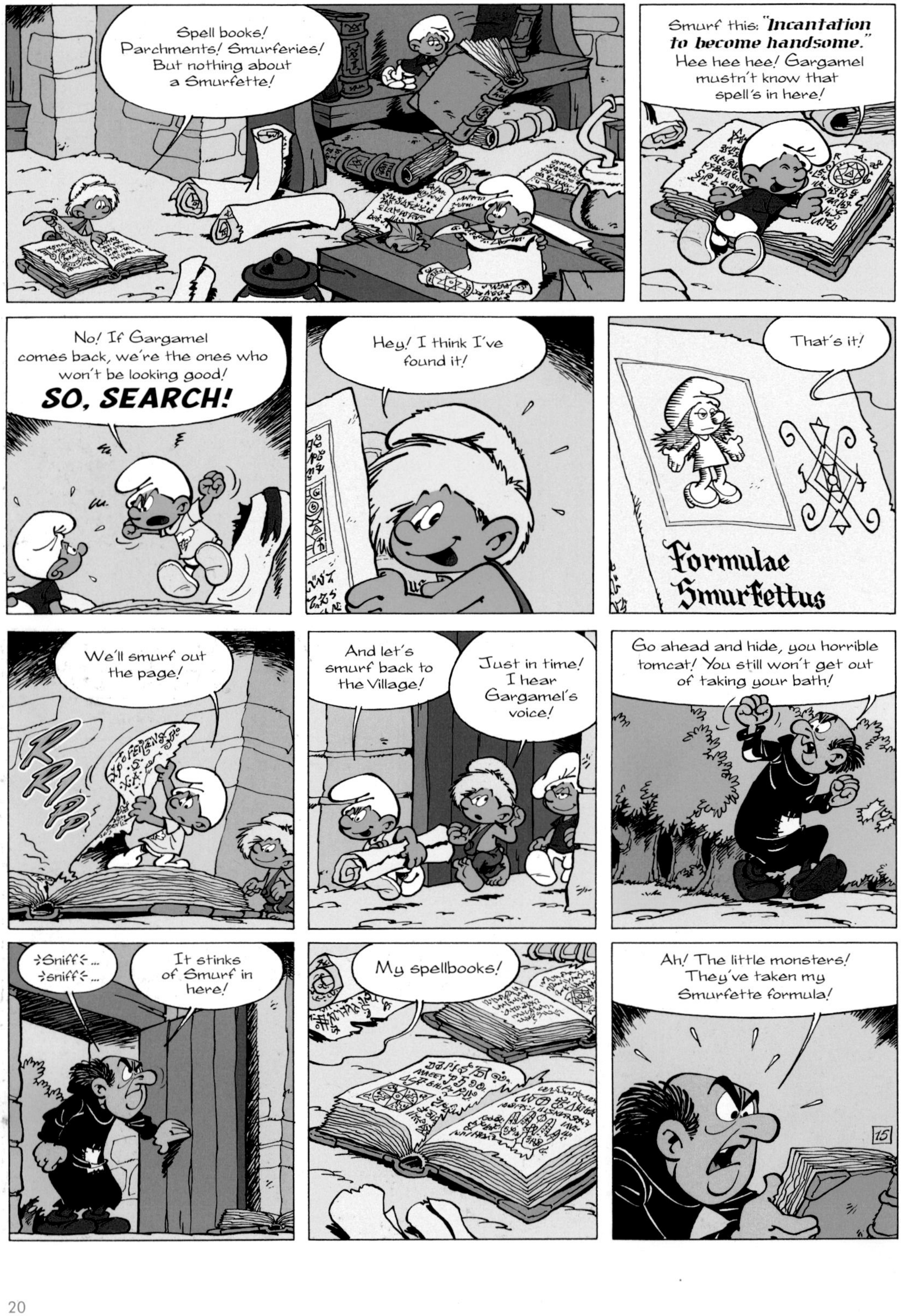
Spell books! Parchments! Smurferies! But nothing about a Smurfette!
Smurf this: "Incantation to become handsome." Hee hee hee! Gargamel mustn't know that spell's in here!
No! If Gargamel comes back, we're the ones who won't be looking good! SO, SEARCH!
Hey! I think I've found it!
That's it!
Formulae Smurfettus
We'll smurf out the page!
RRIPP
And let's smurf back to the Village!
Just in time! I hear Gargamel's voice!
Go ahead and hide, you horrible tomcat! You still won't get out of taking your bath!
Sniff... sniff...
It stinks of Smurf in here!
My spellbooks!
Ah! The little monsters! They've taken my Smurfette formula!
15

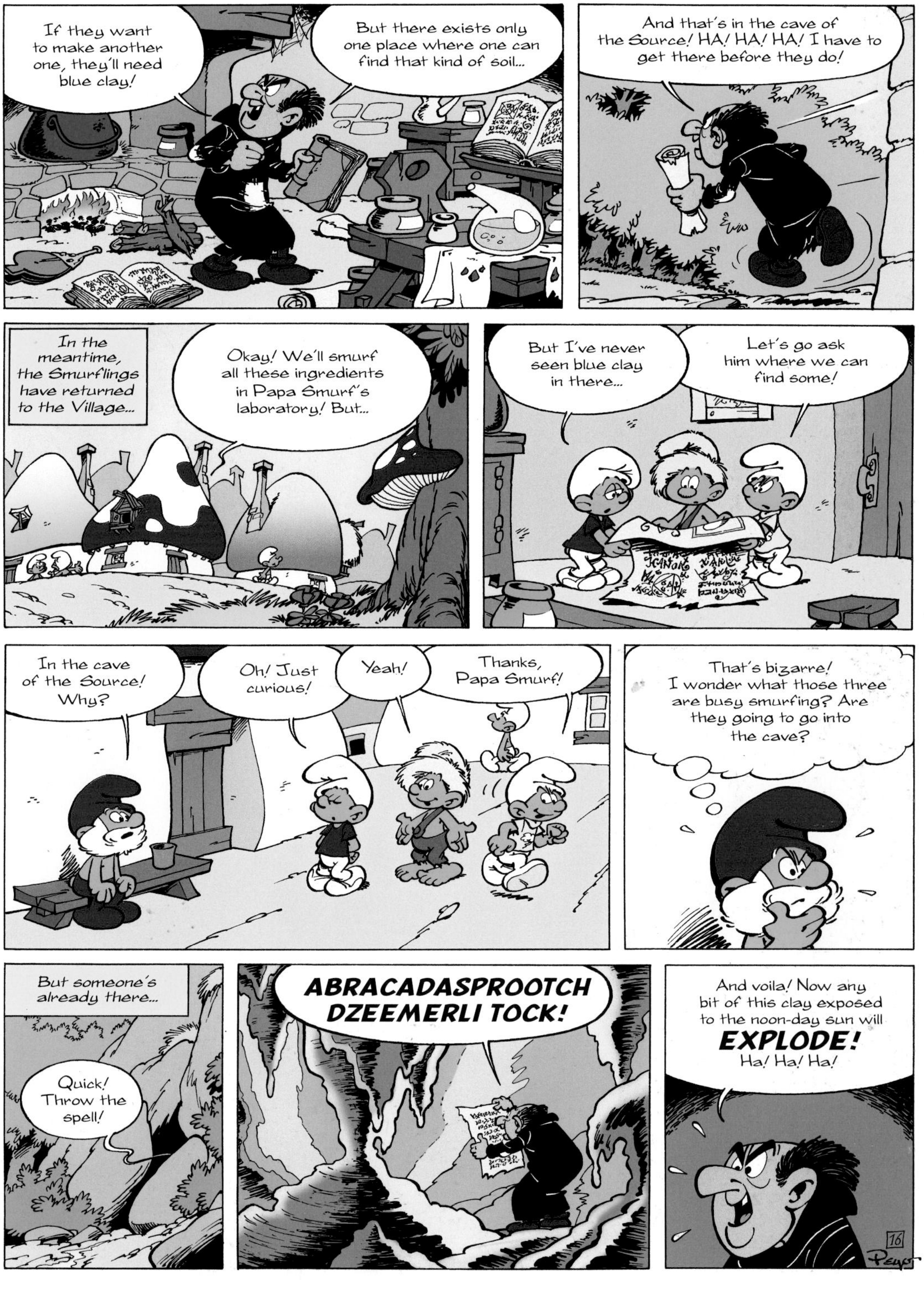
If they want to make another one, they'll need blue clay!
But there exists only one place where one can find that kind of soil...
And that's in the cave of the Source! HA! HA! HA! I have to get there before they do!
In the meantime, the Smurflings have returned to the Village...
Okay! We'll smurf all these ingredients in Papa Smurf's laboratory! But...
But I've never seen blue clay in there...
Let's go ask him where we can find some!
In the cave of the Source! Why?
Oh! Just curious!
Yeah!
Thanks, Papa Smurf!
That's bizarre! I wonder what those three are busy smurfing? Are they going to go into the cave?
But someone's already there...
Quick! Throw the spell!
ABRACADASPROOTCH DZEEMERLI TOCK!
And voila! Now any bit of this clay exposed to the noon-day sun will EXPLODE! Ha! Ha! Ha!
16

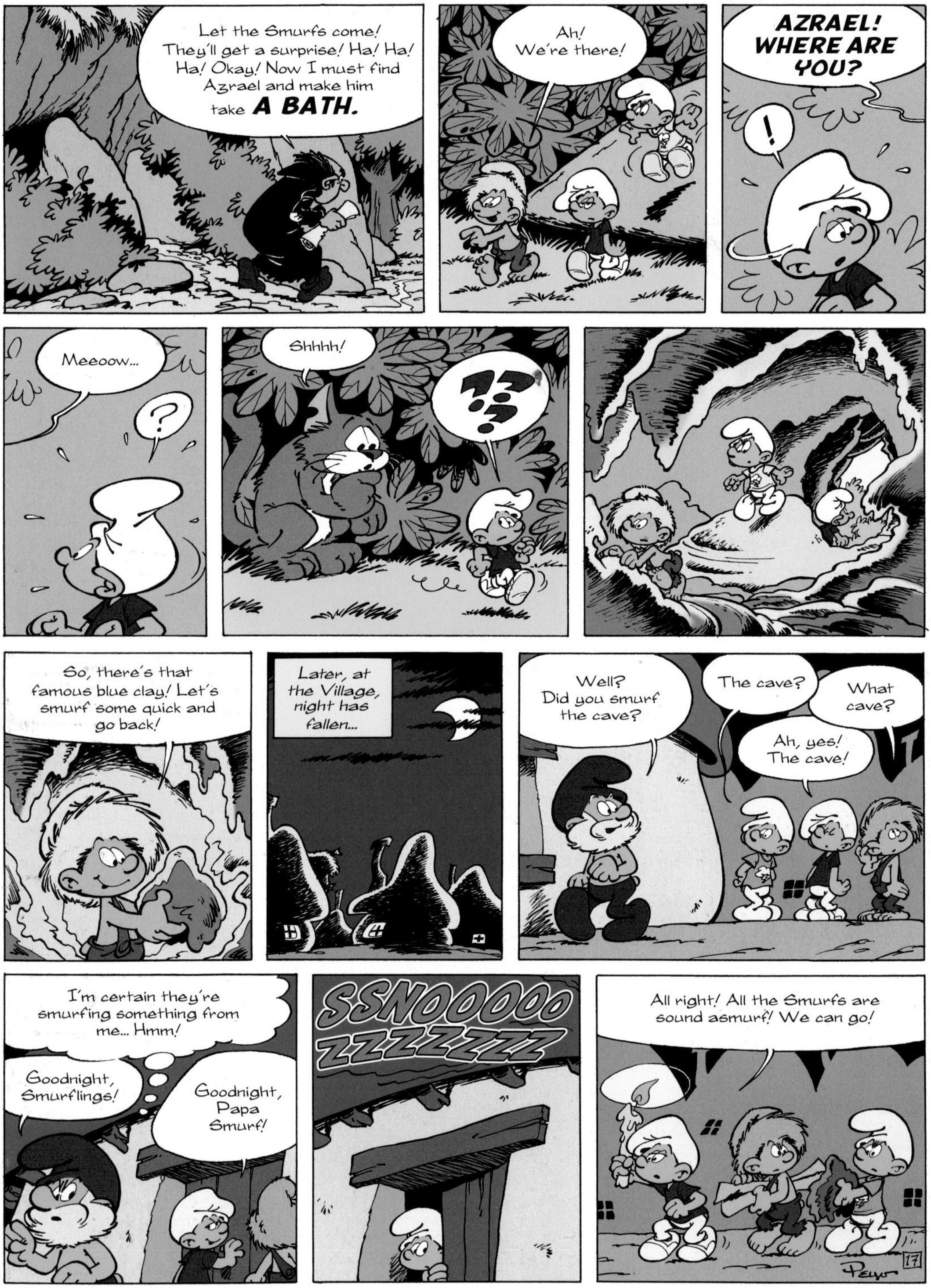
Let the Smurfs come! They'll get a surprise! Ha! Ha! Ha! Okay! Now I must find Azrael and make him take A BATH.
Ah! We're there!
AZRAEL! WHERE ARE YOU?
!
Meeoow...
?
Shhhh!
So, there's that famous blue clay! Let's smurf some quick and go back!
Later, at the Village, night has fallen...
Well? Did you smurf the cave?
The cave?
What cave?
Ah, yes! The cave!
I'm certain they're smurfing something from me... Hmm!
Goodnight, Smurflings!
Goodnight, Papa Smurf!
SSNOOOOOO ZZZZZZZ
All right! All the Smurfs are sound asmurf! We can go!
17
Peyo

Whew! It's open!

Now to work! We have to smurf a fire...

Shape the clay...

Find the right ingredients...

First, fill a basin halfway with water!

Here are all the bottles I smurfed!

How's your modeling smurfing?

Well, it's not easy!

...And the Smurflings work all night long...

Here's the candle!

I have some white thread!

Good!

Z₃₃

Snnrr ZZZZ...

Is the mixture ready?

Yes! We can't smurf it on the fire!

Get smurfing! It'll smurf dawn soon!

Yikes! Pull the basin off! It's boiling! And it mustn't boil!

BLUB BURBLEBURBLE BLUB

Koff koff!

Whew! The smoke's dissipating! I'm curious to see whether--

Hello!

Oh!

Eh!

Hmm...

24

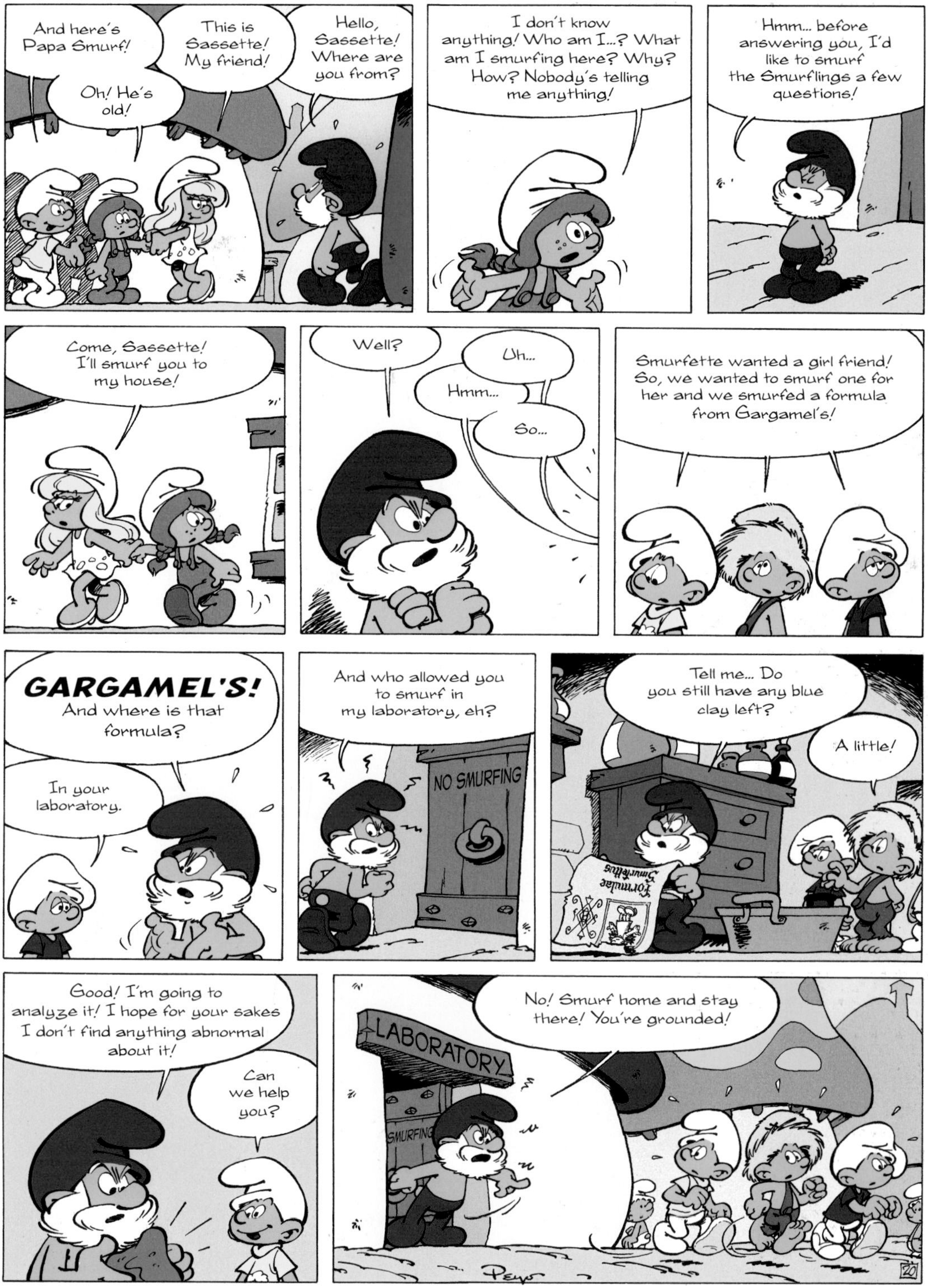
And here's Papa Smurf!
This is Sassette! My friend!
Oh! He's old!
Hello, Sassette! Where are you from?
I don't know anything! Who am I...? What am I smurfing here? Why? How? Nobody's telling me anything!
Hmm... before answering you, I'd like to smurf the Smurflings a few questions!
Come, Sassette! I'll smurf you to my house!
Well?
Uh...
Hmm...
So...
Smurfette wanted a girl friend! So, we wanted to smurf one for her and we smurfed a formula from Gargamel's!
GARGAMEL'S! And where is that formula?
In your laboratory.
And who allowed you to smurf in my laboratory, eh?
NO SMURFING
Tell me... Do you still have any blue clay left?
A little!
Good! I'm going to analyze it! I hope for your sakes I don't find anything abnormal about it!
Can we help you?
LABORATORY
No! Smurf home and stay there! You're grounded!
SMURFING
20

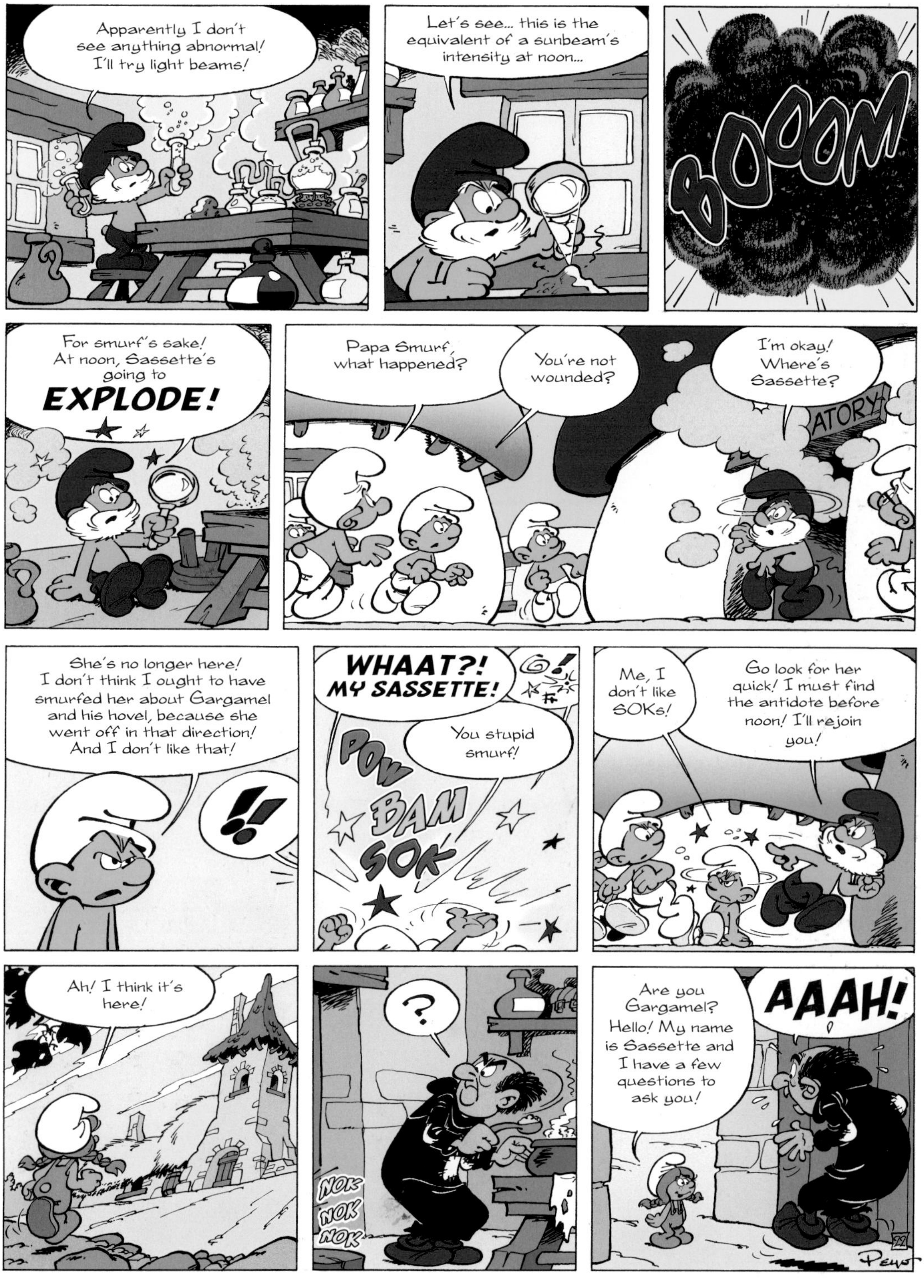

Apparently I don't see anything abnormal! I'll try light beams!
Let's see... this is the equivalent of a sunbeam's intensity at noon...
BOOOOM
For smurf's sake! At noon, Sassette's going to EXPLODE!
Papa Smurf, what happened?
You're not wounded?
I'm okay! Where's Sassette?
ATORY
She's no longer here! I don't think I ought to have smurfed her about Gargamel and his hovel, because she went off in that direction! And I don't like that!
!!
WHAAT?! MY SASSETTE!
You stupid smurf!
POW
BAM
SOK
Me, I don't like SOKs!
Go look for her quick! I must find the antidote before noon! I'll rejoin you!
Ah! I think it's here!
?
NOK
NOK
NOK
Are you Gargamel? Hello! My name is Sassette and I have a few questions to ask you!
AAAH!

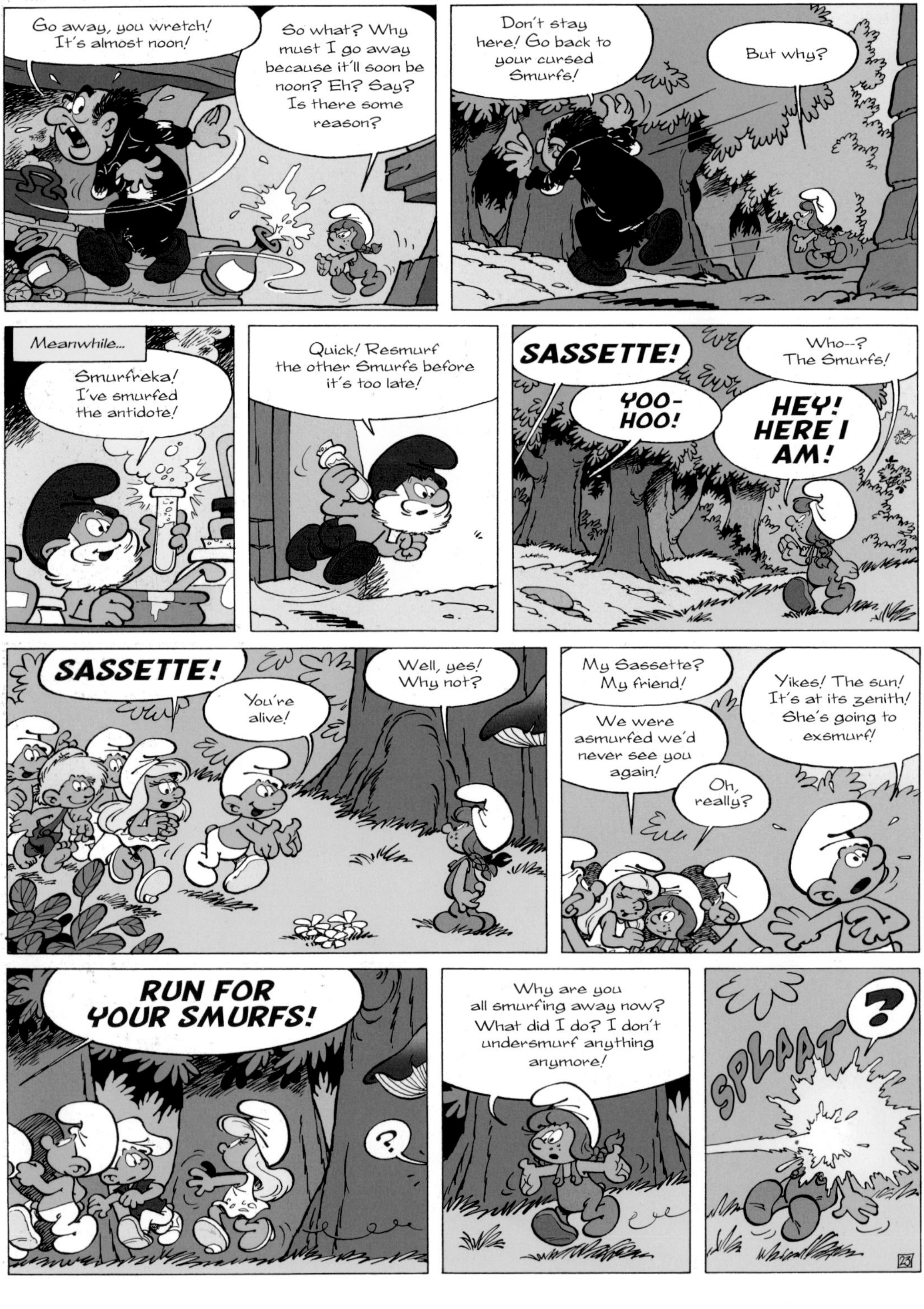
Go away, you wretch! It's almost noon!
So what? Why must I go away because it'll soon be noon? Eh? Say? Is there some reason?
Don't stay here! Go back to your cursed Smurfs!
But why?
Meanwhile...
Smurfreka! I've smurfed the antidote!
Quick! Resmurf the other Smurfs before it's too late!
SASSETTE!
YOO-HOO!
Who--? The Smurfs!
HEY! HERE I AM!
SASSETTE!
You're alive!
Well, yes! Why not?
My Sassette? My friend!
We were asmurfed we'd never see you again!
Oh, really?
Yikes! The sun! It's at its zenith! She's going to exsmurf!
RUN FOR YOUR SMURFS!
?
Why are you all smurfing away now? What did I do? I don't undersmurf anything anymore!
SPLAAT
?
23

THE END

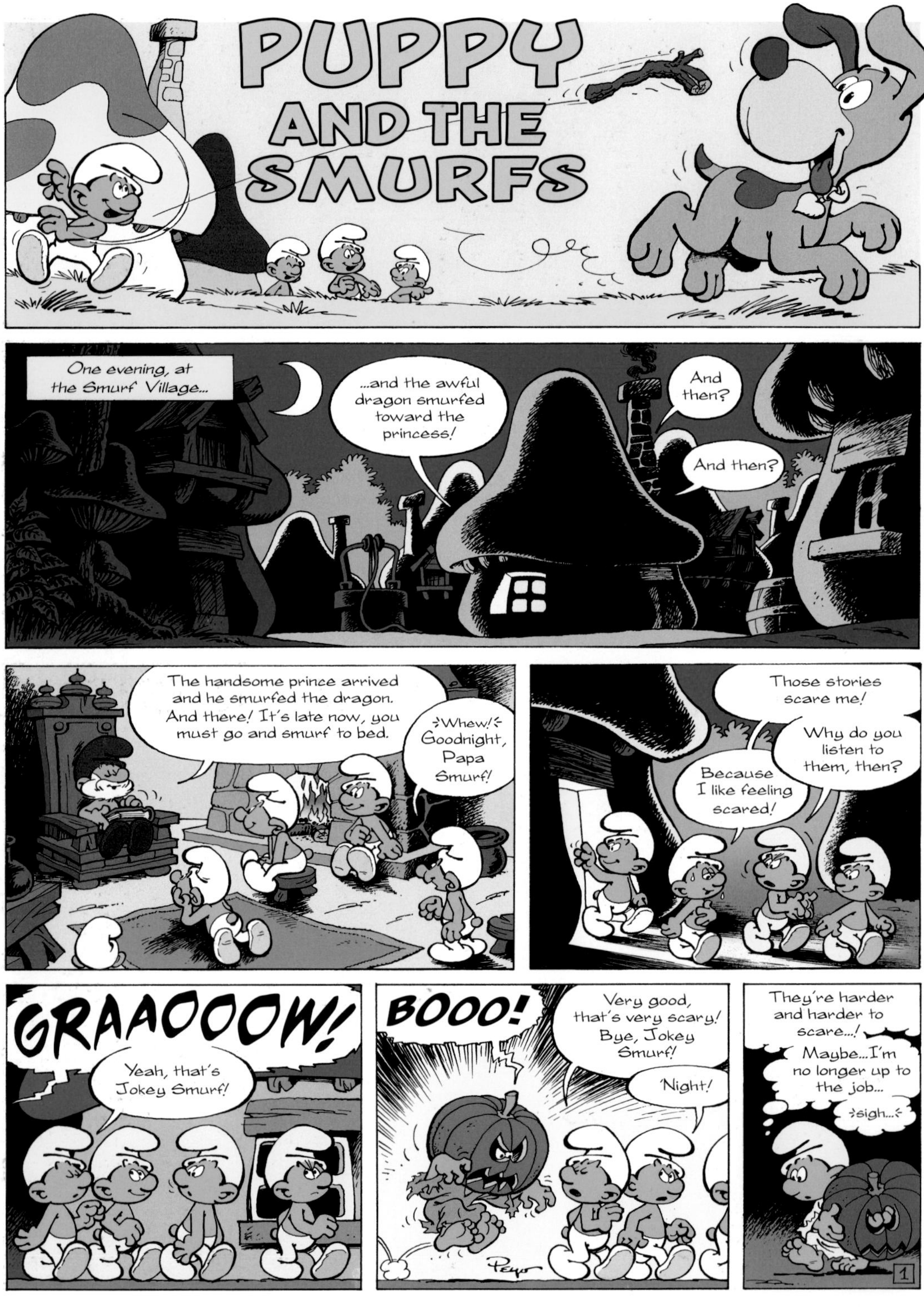
PUPPY AND THE SMURFS
One evening, at the Smurf Village...
...and the awful dragon smurfed toward the princess!
And then?
And then?
The handsome prince arrived and he smurfed the dragon. And there! It's late now, you must go and smurf to bed.
Whew! Goodnight, Papa Smurf!
Those stories scare me!
Why do you listen to them, then?
Because I like feeling scared!
GRAAOOOW!
Yeah, that's Jokey Smurf!
BOOO!
Very good, that's very scary! Bye, Jokey Smurf!
'Night!
They're harder and harder to scare...!
Maybe...I'm no longer up to the job...
sigh...
Peyo
1

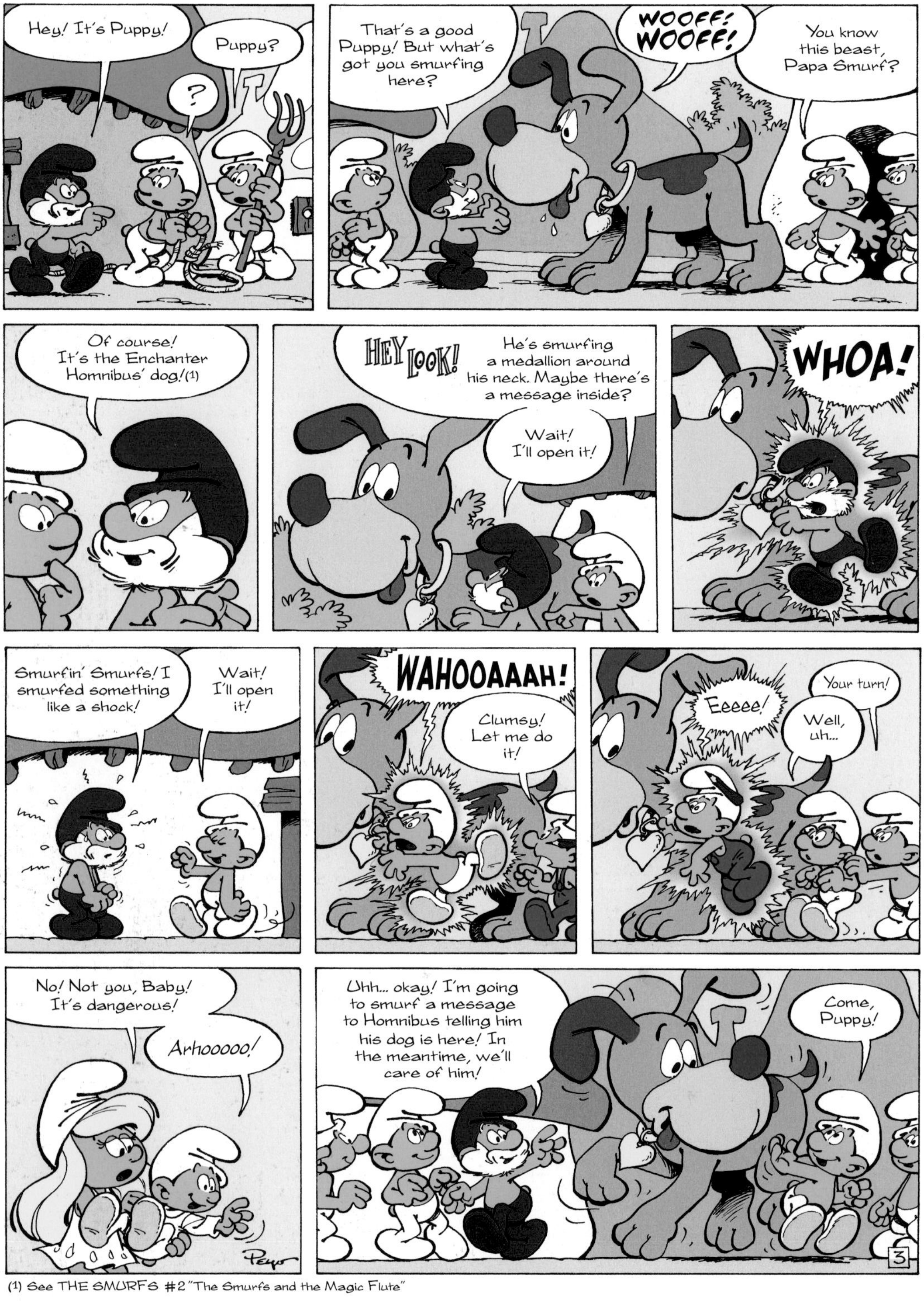
Hey! It's Puppy!
Puppy?
?
That's a good Puppy! But what's got you smurfing here?
WOOFF! WOOFF!
You know this beast, Papa Smurf?
Of course! It's the Enchanter Homnibus' dog!(1)
HEY LOOK!
He's smurfing a medallion around his neck. Maybe there's a message inside?
Wait! I'll open it!
WHOA!
Smurfin' Smurfs! I smurfed something like a shock!
Wait! I'll open it!
WAHOOAAAH!
Clumsy! Let me do it!
Eeeee!
Your turn!
Well, uh...
No! Not you, Baby! It's dangerous!
Arhooooo!
Uhh... okay! I'm going to smurf a message to Homnibus telling him his dog is here! In the meantime, we'll care of him!
Come, Puppy!
Peyo
3

(1) See THE SMURFS #2 "The Smurfs and the Magic Flute"

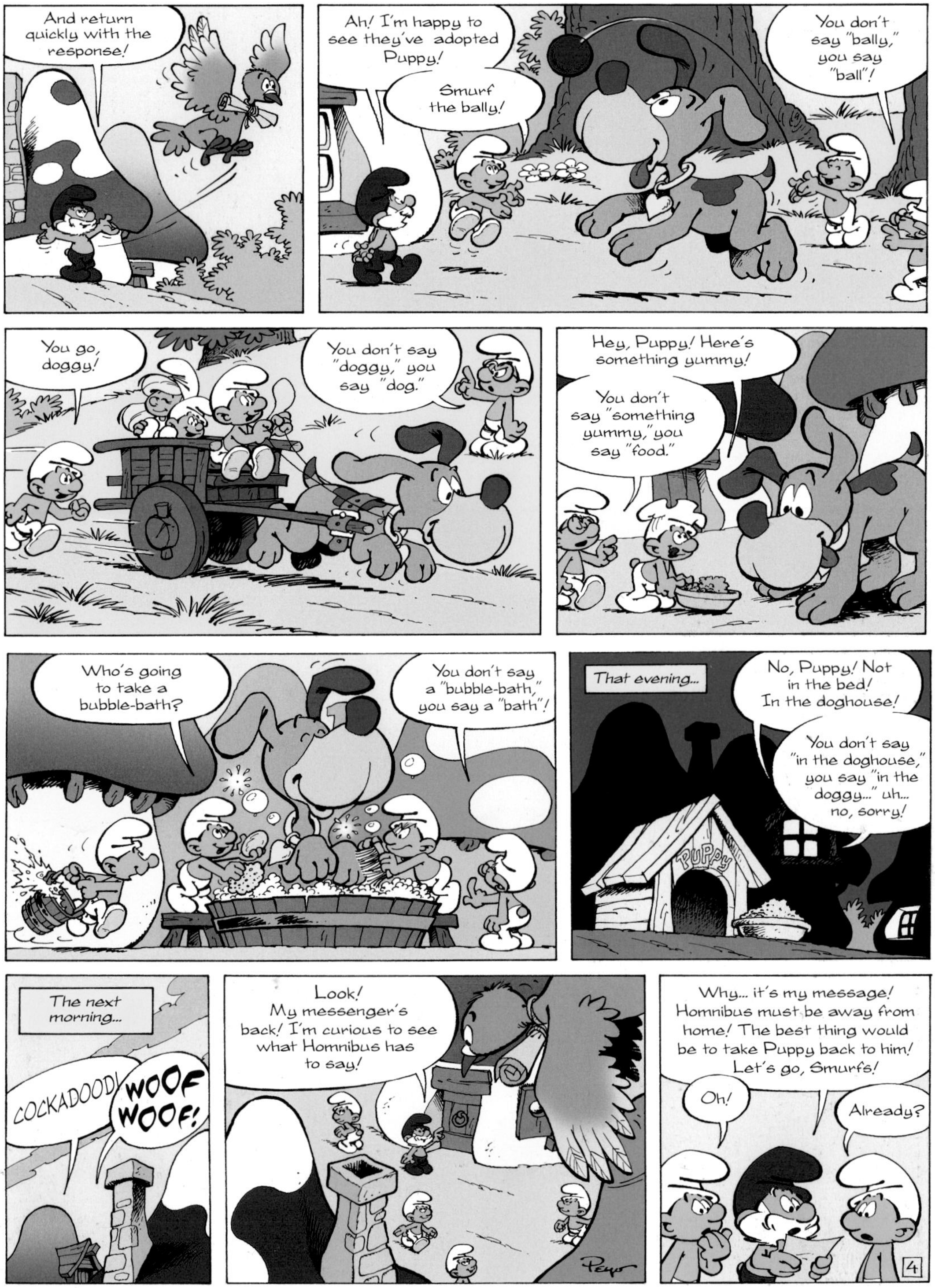
And return quickly with the response!
Ah! I'm happy to see they've adopted Puppy!
Smurf the bally!
You don't say "bally," you say "ball"!
You go, doggy!
You don't say "doggy," you say "dog."
Hey, Puppy! Here's something yummy!
You don't say "something yummy," you say "food."
Who's going to take a bubble-bath?
You don't say a "bubble-bath," you say a "bath"!
That evening...
No, Puppy! Not in the bed! In the doghouse!
You don't say "in the doghouse," you say "in the doggy..." uh... no, sorry!
PUPPY
The next morning...
COCKADOODL
WOOF WOOF!
Look! My messenger's back! I'm curious to see what Homnibus has to say!
Peyo
Why... it's my message! Homnibus must be away from home! The best thing would be to take Puppy back to him! Let's go, Smurfs!
Oh!
Already?
4

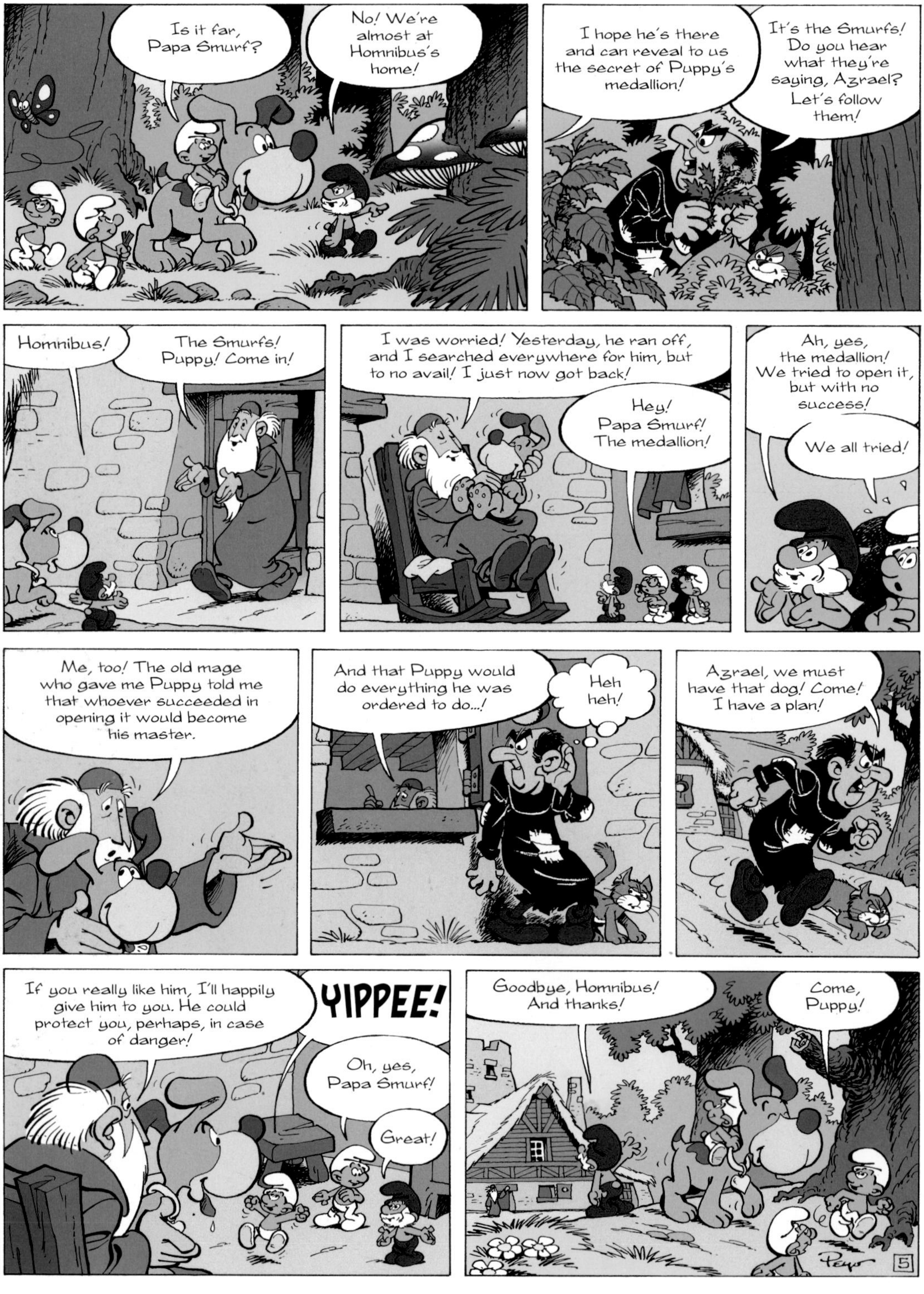

Is it far, Papa Smurf?
No! We're almost at Homnibus's home!
I hope he's there and can reveal to us the secret of Puppy's medallion!
It's the Smurfs! Do you hear what they're saying, Azrael? Let's follow them!
Homnibus!
The Smurfs! Puppy! Come in!
I was worried! Yesterday, he ran off, and I searched everywhere for him, but to no avail! I just now got back!
Hey! Papa Smurf! The medallion!
Ah, yes, the medallion! We tried to open it, but with no success!
We all tried!
Me, too! The old mage who gave me Puppy told me that whoever succeeded in opening it would become his master.
And that Puppy would do everything he was ordered to do...!
Heh heh!
Azrael, we must have that dog! Come! I have a plan!
If you really like him, I'll happily give him to you. He could protect you, perhaps, in case of danger!
YIPPEE!
Oh, yes, Papa Smurf!
Great!
Goodbye, Homnibus! And thanks!
Come, Puppy!
Peyo
5

35

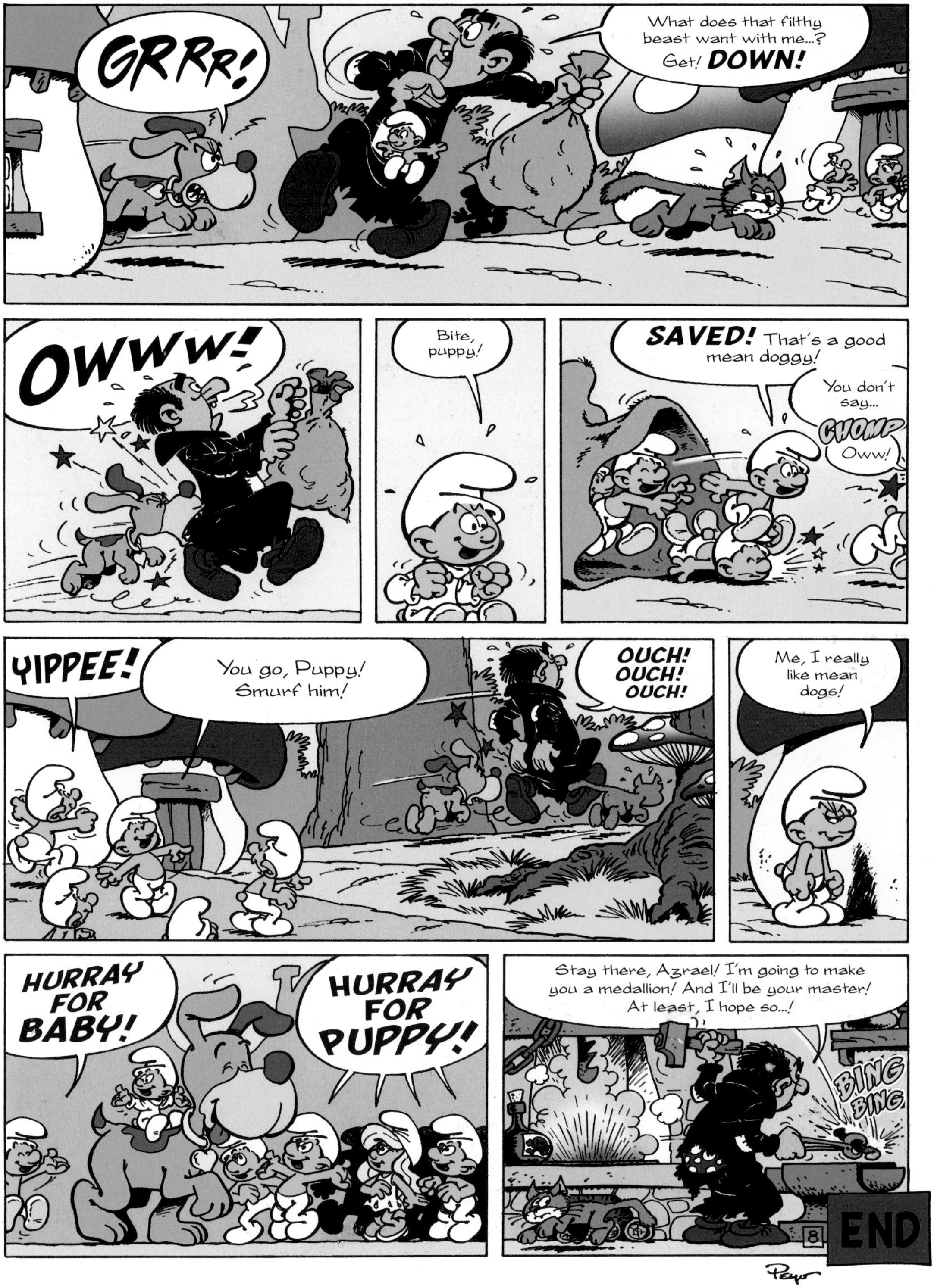
GRRRR!
What does that filthy beast want with me...? Get! DOWN!
OWWW!
Bite, puppy!
SAVED! That's a good mean doggy!
You don't say...
CHOMP
Oww!
YIPPEE!
You go, Puppy! Smurf him!
OUCH! OUCH! OUCH!
Me, I really like mean dogs!
HURRAY FOR BABY!
HURRAY FOR PUPPY!
Stay there, Azrael! I'm going to make you a medallion! And I'll be your master! At least, I hope so...!
BING BING
8
END
Peyo

THE SMURFS AND THE LITTLE GHOSTS

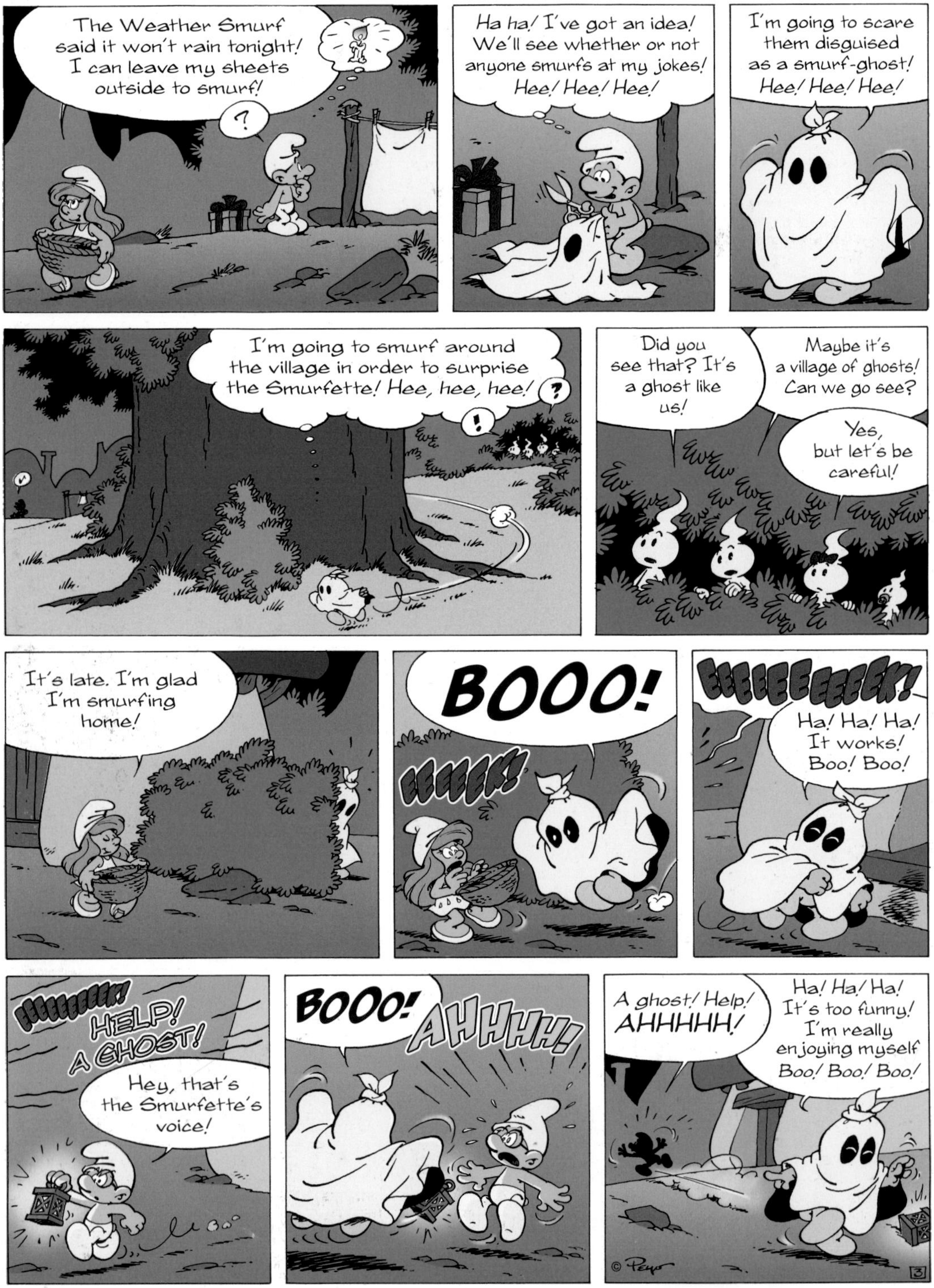

The Weather Smurf said it won't rain tonight! I can leave my sheets outside to smurf!
?
Ha ha! I've got an idea! We'll see whether or not anyone smurfs at my jokes! Hee! Hee! Hee!
I'm going to scare them disguised as a smurf-ghost! Hee! Hee! Hee!
I'm going to smurf around the village in order to surprise the Smurfette! Hee, hee, hee!
?
!
Did you see that? It's a ghost like us!
Maybe it's a village of ghosts! Can we go see?
Yes, but let's be careful!
It's late. I'm glad I'm smurfing home!
BOOO!
EEEEEK!
EEEEEEEEEEK!
Ha! Ha! Ha! It works! Boo! Boo!
EEEEEEEEEK!
HELP! A GHOST!
Hey, that's the Smurfette's voice!
BOOO!
AHHHHH!
A ghost! Help! AHHHHH!
Ha! Ha! Ha! It's too funny! I'm really enjoying myself Boo! Boo! Boo!
© Peyo
3

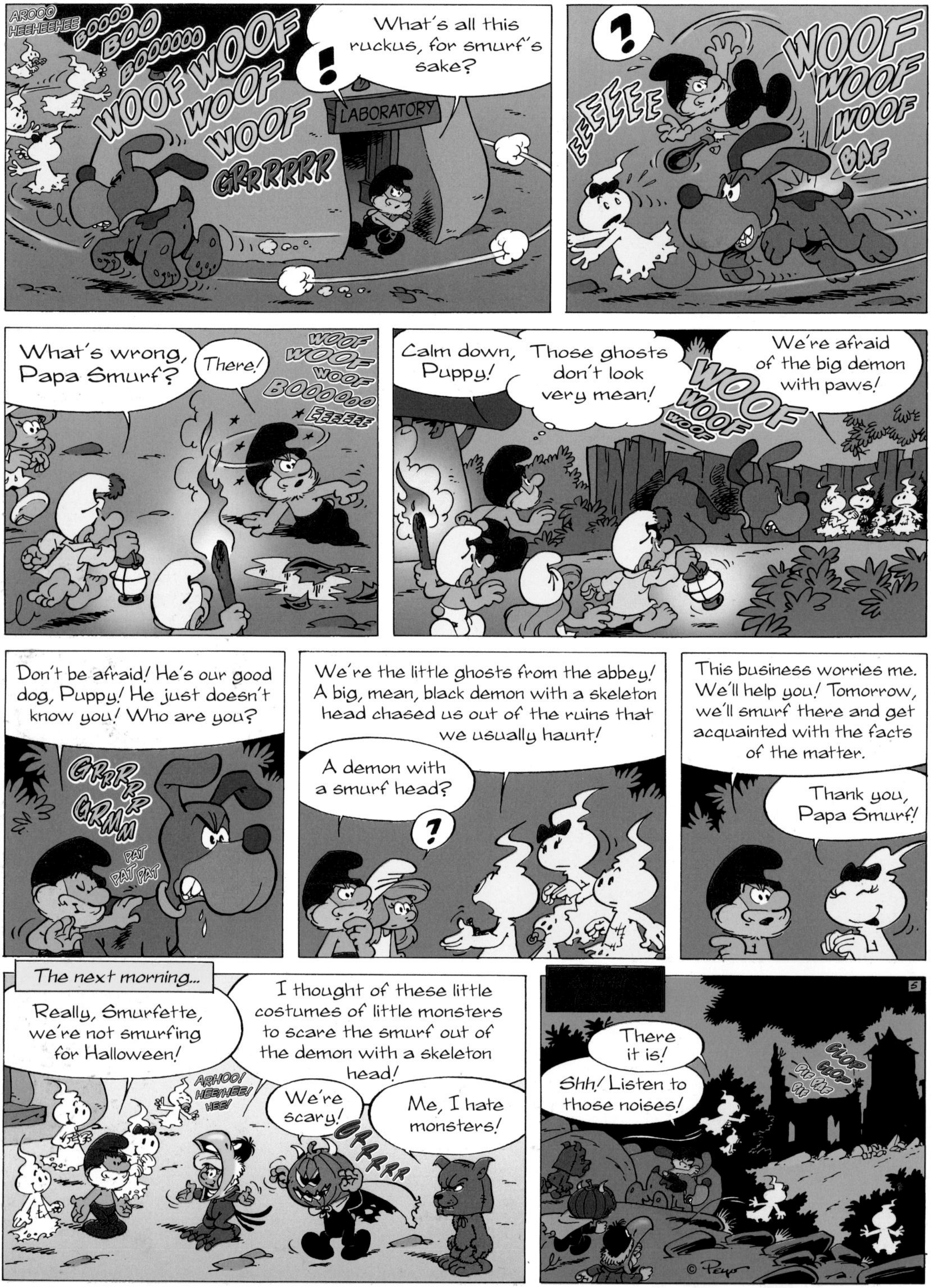
ARDOO HEEHEEHEE
BOOOO
BOO
BOOOOOO
WOOF WOOF
WOOF
WOOF
GRRRRRR
What's all this ruckus, for smurf's sake?
!
LABORATORY
?
EEEEEE
WOOF
WOOF
WOOF
BAF
What's wrong, Papa Smurf?
There!
WOOF
WOOF
WOOF
BOOOOooo
EEEEEE
Calm down, Puppy!
Those ghosts don't look very mean!
We're afraid of the big demon with paws!
WOOF
WOOF
WOOF
Don't be afraid! He's our good dog, Puppy! He just doesn't know you! Who are you?
GRRRRR
GRMM
PAT
PAT PAT
We're the little ghosts from the abbey! A big, mean, black demon with a skeleton head chased us out of the ruins that we usually haunt!
A demon with a smurf head?
?
This business worries me. We'll help you! Tomorrow, we'll smurf there and get acquainted with the facts of the matter.
Thank you, Papa Smurf!
The next morning...
Really, Smurfette, we're not smurfing for Halloween!
I thought of these little costumes of little monsters to scare the smurf out of the demon with a skeleton head!
ARHOO! HEEHEE! HEE!
We're scary!
GRRRRR
Me, I hate monsters!
5
There it is!
Shh! Listen to those noises!
© Peyo

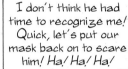

43

44

Let's flee! The bailiff doesn't like sorcerers or demons!

OWW!

We captured them, sir!

No funny business! I'm not afraid of you demons!

?!?

We must set an example! Tie those two jokers in the branches of that apple tree and forget about them!

Amen!

The bailiff's soldiers are smurfing this way!

Follow me with your little ghosts. I know a place you can haunt in complete safety!

That old tower has been abandoned for ages! You can smurf there in peace!

Thank you, Papa Smurf!

HURRAH!

BOOO

It's our new home, baby!

It's time to smurf back to the village!

Goodbye! BOOOOOOOO

Good luck!

Hee, hee, the Bailiff has smurfed Gargamel in the branches of the apple tree!

Get out of here! I'm a demon! ARHH ARHH!

SPLOTCH!

SPLAT

RIGHT SMACK ON HIS SMURF!

HEE! HEE! HA! HA! HA!

SPLAT.

Cursed Smurfs! You'll pay for that a hundred-fold! ARHHHHH!

© Peyo

THE END.

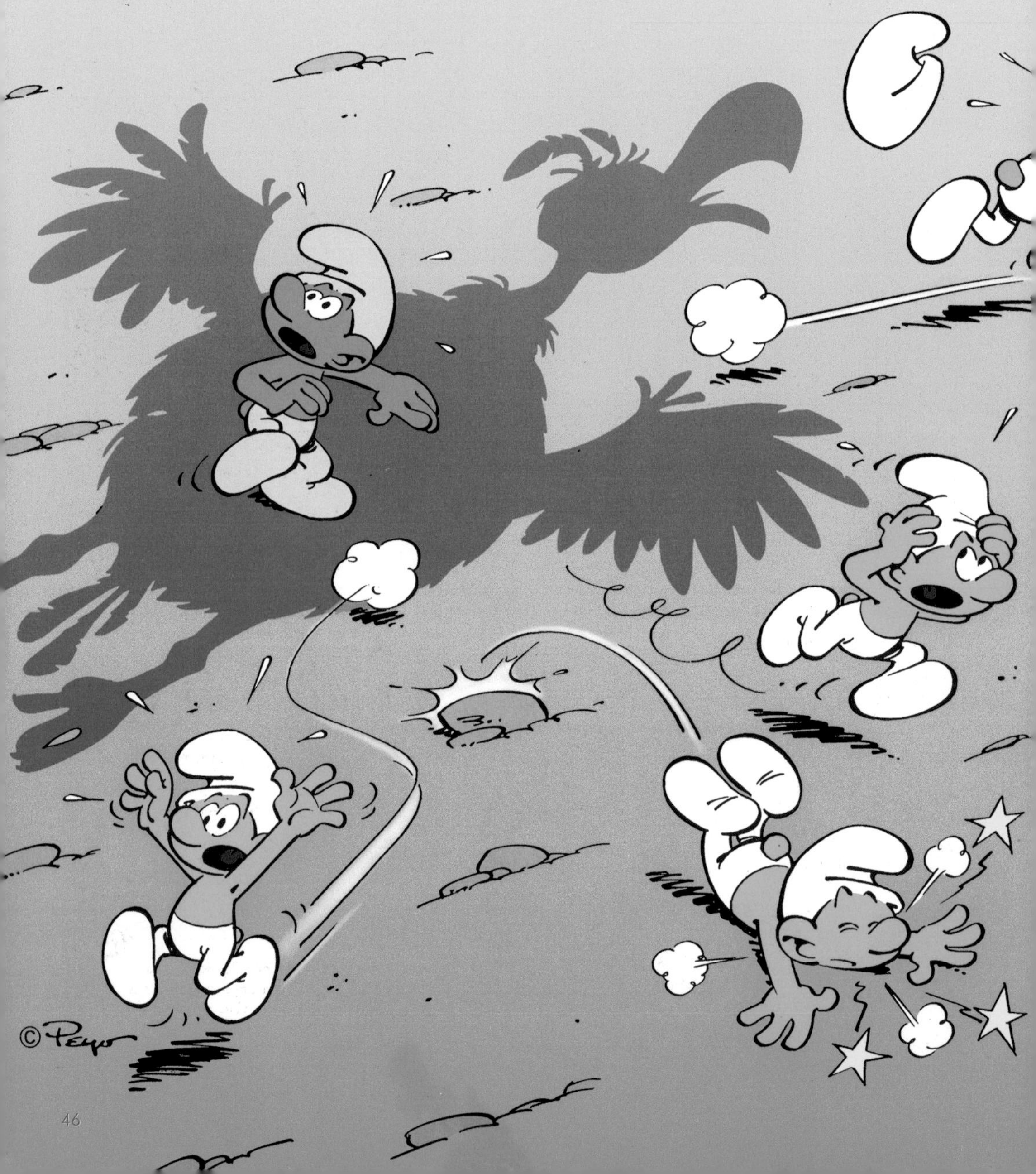
© Peyo

THE SMURFS AND THE BOOGLOOBOO

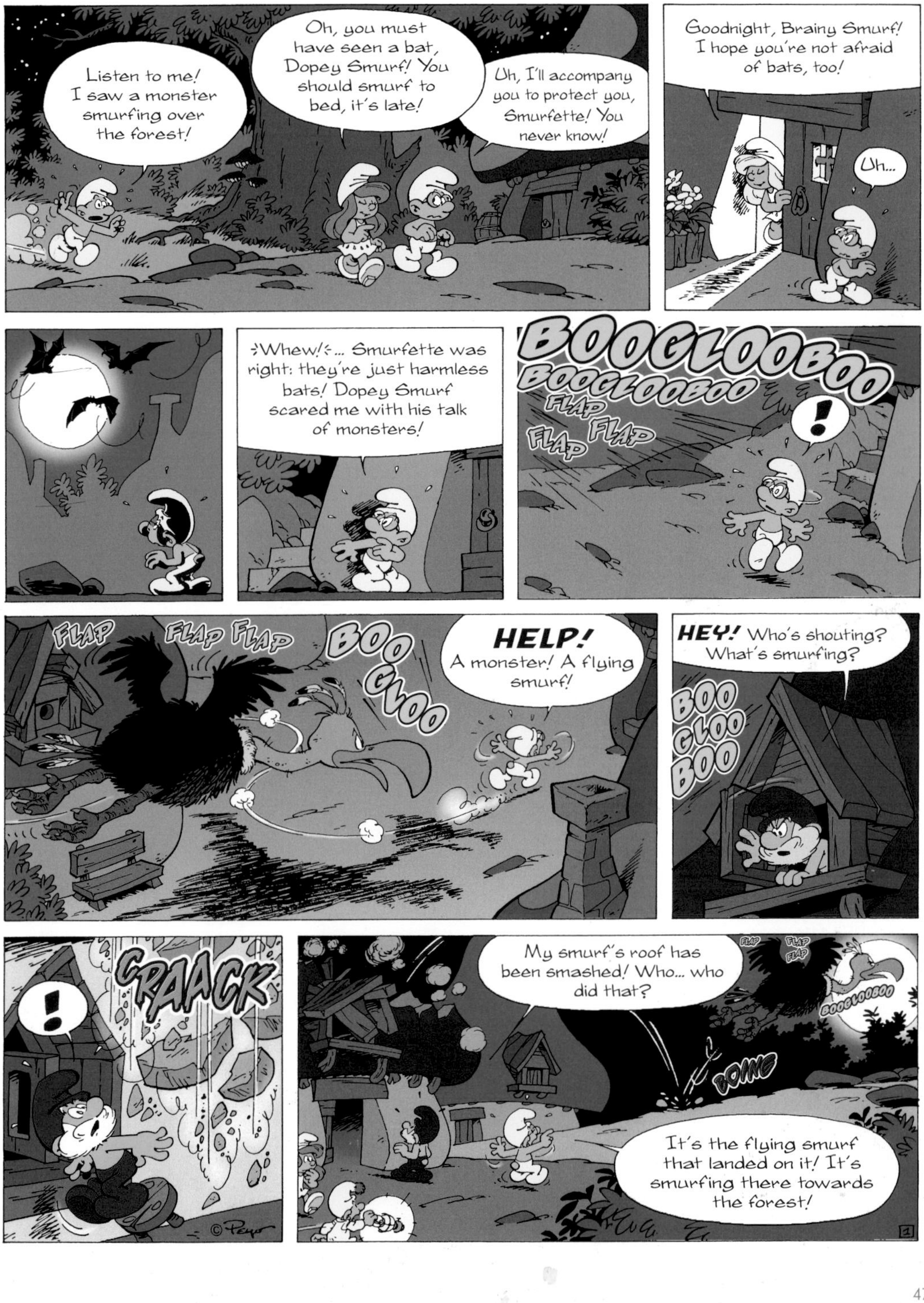

Listen to me! I saw a monster smurfing over the forest!
Oh, you must have seen a bat, Dopey Smurf! You should smurf to bed, it's late!
Uh, I'll accompany you to protect you, Smurfette! You never know!
Goodnight, Brainy Smurf! I hope you're not afraid of bats, too!
Uh...
Whew!... Smurfette was right: they're just harmless bats! Dopey Smurf scared me with his talk of monsters!
BOOGLOOBOO
BOOGLOOBOO
FLAP
FLAP
FLAP
!
FLAP
FLAP FLAP
BOO GLOO
HELP! A monster! A flying smurf!
HEY! Who's shouting? What's smurfing?
BOO GLOO BOO
CRAACK
!
© Peyo
My smurf's roof has been smashed! Who... who did that?
FLAP
FLAP FLAP
BOOGLOOBOO
BOING
It's the flying smurf that landed on it! It's smurfing there towards the forest!
1

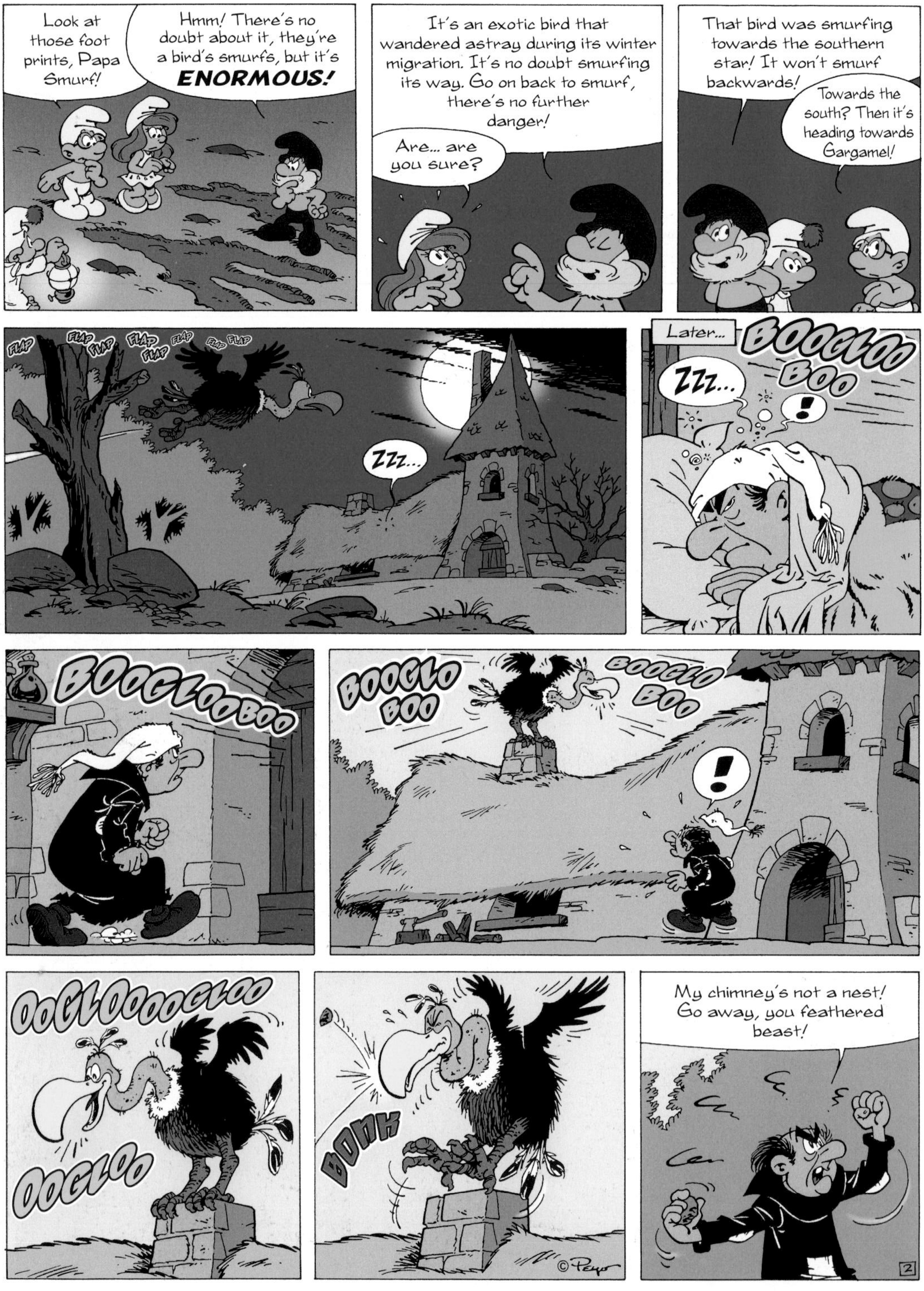
Look at those foot prints, Papa Smurf!
Hmm! There's no doubt about it, they're a bird's smurfs, but it's ENORMOUS!
It's an exotic bird that wandered astray during its winter migration. It's no doubt smurfing its way. Go on back to smurf, there's no further danger!
Are... are you sure?
That bird was smurfing towards the southern star! It won't smurf backwards!
Towards the south? Then it's heading towards Gargamel!
FLAP FLAP FLAP FLAP FLAP FLAP FLAP FLAP
ZZZ...
Later...
BOOGLOO BOO
ZZZ...
!
BOOGLOOBOO
BOOGLO BOO
BOOGLO BOO
!
OOGLOOOOOGLOO
OOGLOO
BONK
© Peyo
My chimney's not a nest! Go away, you feathered beast!
2

That afternoon...

Ah, it's leaving its nest! Now's my chance...!

I'll demolish it all! Then I'll start a fire in the chimney! That wretched bird won't ever come back! Ha ha!

What?! There's an egg in this nest!

!

BOOGLOOBEE BOOGLOOBEE

BOOGLOOBOO

Gulp!

BOOGLOOBEE BOOGLOOBEE!!

OW! LET ME GO!

AAAAA!

FLAP FLAP FLAP FLAP FLAP

Just great! I get it: the mother's telling me to keep away from her baby! Getting rid of them won't be easy!

FLAP FLAP FLAP FLAP

OOGVOO

BOOGLI!!

BOOOOO!!

NIBBLE NIBBLE CHOMP

She feeds snakes to her baby! Yuck!

CHOMP MUNCH CHOMP CHOMP! BOOGLOO BOO CLOOBOO

© Peyo

4

At the same moment...

Yes, I swear to you I heard the Booglooboo's cry this morning, near the snake pond!

That can't be. Papa Smurf said that migratory smurfs smurfed towards the south and never went backwards--

BOOGLOO BOO

There! It sounds like it's coming from Gargamel's home!

HMMLOOBOO GLOOBOO BOO GLOO

You see-- I was right!

BOOGLOO FLAP FLAP FLAP FLAP FLAP BOOGLEEEE

There's a baby! The mother's smurfing the nest!

Watch out! Gargamel's smurfing behind that wall!

Heh heh heh!

Ha! Ha! Now I've got you! I'm going to get rid of you and your mama too!

BOGOOORR!!

I'll dump you in the forest! Your mama won't ever find you and will leave my house! Heh heh heh!

BOOGLOO BEEEEE

He smurfed the baby into a sack!

After them! We must smurf the baby!

That's not safe and-- Wait for me!

BYE-BYE, BIRDIE!

BOOGLEEE VOOM

BOINK

NO!

SPLOOSH

You're safe, Baby Booglooboo!

Calm down! Don't be afraid!

© Peyo

5

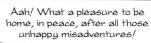

WATCH OUT FOR PAPERCUTZ ™

Welcome to the forever-young fifteenth SMURFS graphic novel by Peyo from Papercutz, the little company dedicated to publishing great graphic novels for all ages. I'm Jim Salicrup, the Smurf-in-Chief, with another exciting Peyo-related announcement.

As I'm sure you'll recall from THE SMURFS #14 "The Baby Smurf," we talked about 2013 shaping up as quite possibly the Smurfiest year ever! What with the all-new SMURFS 2 movie from Sony Pictures Animation, coming to a theater near you July 2013, as well as BENNY BREAKIRON, a new Papercutz graphic novel series, created by Peyo, featuring the fun-filled adventures of a super-powered little French boy, that's available now at your favorite booksellers. And the BIG NEWS this time around is that Papercutz will be publishing another new Peyo series—THE SMURFS ANTHOLOGY!

Available in deluxe hardcover editions, THE SMURFS ANTHOLOGY will feature all the original Peyo Smurfs comics, in the order they were originally published in Europe. But that's not all— each 192-page volume of THE SMURFS ANTHOLOGY will also feature the JOHAN AND PEEWIT comics, in which the Smurfs originally appeared. You remember Johan and Peewit from THE SMURFS #2 "The Smurfs and the Magic Flute," right? That's where we also met Homnibus the Enchanter, who's back for a cameo appearance in this very volume. Well, there were a few more Johan and Peewit adventures that guest-starred the Smurfs, that haven't been published before by Papercutz, so these comics will be collected exclusively in THE SMURFS ANTHOLOGY. Coming in June 2013, we're sure no Blue-Believer will want to miss THE SMURFS ANTHOLOGY.

In the meantime, the Smurfiness continues here too! Coming soon is THE SMURFS #16 "The Aerosmurf," the long-awaited sequel to "The Flying Smurf" story that appeared in THE SMURFS #1 "The Purple Smurfs." Finally, the Smurf who dreamed of flying finally gets his wish—but when his flying somehow results in Smurfette getting captured by Gargamel, it's up to him to rescue her!

STAY IN TOUCH!
EMAIL: Salicrup@papercutz.com
WEB: www.papercutz.com
TWITTER: @papercutzgn
FACEBOOK: PAPERCUTZGRAPHICNOVELS
SNAIL MAIL: Papercutz, 160 Broadway,
  Suite 700, East Wing, New York, NY 10038

Yes, 2013 is truly a very Smurfy year!
Smurf you later!

Jim